INDUSTRIAL PHARMACY-II

For
Third Year B. Pharm. Course
Semester - VI

Dr. Vrushali S. Kashikar (Kulkarni)
(M.Pharm., Ph.D.)
Associate Professor & Head,
Dept. of Pharmaceutics,
Modern College of Pharmacy (L),
Moshi, Pune-412105.

Dr. Amol A. Kulkarni
(M.Pharm., Ph.D.)
Associate Professor & Head PG Department,
CAYMET's Siddhant College of Pharmacy,
Pune-412109.

Dr. Indrajeet D. Gonjari
(M.Pharm., Ph.D.)
Assistant Professor
(Former Assistant Director, AICTE, New Delhi)
Government College of Pharmacy,
Ratnagiri.

NIRALI PRAKASHAN
ADVANCEMENT OF KNOWLEDGE

N1707

INDUSTRIAL PHARMACY-II　　　　　　　　　　**ISBN – 978-93-86353-15-3**

First Edition　:　**January 2017**

©　:　**Authors**

Published By :　　　　　　　　　　**Polyplate**

NIRALI PRAKASHAN

Abhyudaya Pragati, 1312, Shivaji Nagar,
Off J.M. Road, Pune – 411005
Tel - (020) 25512336/37/39, Fax - (020) 25511379
Email : niralipune@pragationline.com

☞ **DISTRIBUTION CENTRES**

PUNE

Nirali Prakashan　:　119, Budhwar Peth, Jogeshwari Mandir Lane, Pune 411002, Maharashtra
Tel : (020) 2445 2044, 66022708, Fax : (020) 2445 1538
Email : bookorder@pragationline.com, niralilocal@pragationline.com

Nirali Prakashan　:　S. No. 28/27, Dhyari, Near Pari Company, Pune 411041
Tel : (020) 24690204 Fax : (020) 24690316
Email : dhyari@pragationline.com, bookorder@pragationline.com

MUMBAI

Nirali Prakashan　:　385, S.V.P. Road, Rasdhara Co-op. Hsg. Society Ltd.,
Girgaum, Mumbai 400004, Maharashtra
Tel : (022) 2385 6339 / 2386 9976, Fax : (022) 2386 9976
Email : niralimumbai@pragationline.com

☞ **DISTRIBUTION BRANCHES**

JALGAON

Nirali Prakashan　:　34, V. V. Golani Market, Navi Peth, Jalgaon 425001,
Maharashtra, Tel : (0257) 222 0395, Mob : 94234 91860

KOLHAPUR

Nirali Prakashan　:　New Mahadvar Road, Kedar Plaza, 1st Floor Opp. IDBI Bank
Kolhapur 416 012, Maharashtra. Mob : 9850046155

NAGPUR

Pratibha Book Distributors　:　Above Maratha Mandir, Shop No. 3, First Floor,
Rani Jhanshi Square, Sitabuldi, Nagpur 440012, Maharashtra
Tel : (0712) 254 7129

DELHI

Nirali Prakashan　:　4593/21, Basement, Aggarwal Lane 15, Ansari Road, Daryaganj
Near Times of India Building, New Delhi 110002
Mob : 08505972553

BENGALURU

Pragati Book House　:　House No. 1, Sanjeevappa Lane, Avenue Road Cross,
Opp. Rice Church, Bengaluru – 560002.
Tel : (080) 64513344, 64513355,Mob : 9880582331, 9845021552
Email:bharatsavla@yahoo.com

CHENNAI

Pragati Books　:　9/1, Montieth Road, Behind Taas Mahal, Egmore,
Chennai 600008 Tamil Nadu, Tel : (044) 6518 3535,
Mob : 94440 01782 / 98450 21552 / 98805 82331,
Email : bharatsavla@yahoo.com

niralipune@pragationline.com　|　www.pragationline.com

Also find us on 🅵 www.facebook.com/niralibooks

Dedicated

To

Our

Beloved

Family

Preface

It is our immense pleasure to present a book of **'Industrial Pharmacy-II'**, Semester VI (Third Year), B. Pharm course of Savitribai Phule Pune University. The insight behind publishing this book is to enlighten the students and to fulfill the needs as per the demand of syllabus framed for Industrial Pharmacy-II, Semester VI, B. Pharm course by Savitribai Phule Pune University.

This book covers all the topics of Industrial Pharmacy-II, Semester VI, B. Pharm course. Each topic in the book is supported with frequently asked and repeated questions in the previous annual theory question papers.

As well said that "The good life is one inspired by love and guided by knowledge", this book is a positive outcome of teaching and learning experiences of the authors with the students of Third year B. Pharm course for last 10-12 years.

Your co-operation in the form of suggestions are most welcome for the improvement of the contents of this book in due benefits of pharmacy students in further editions.

December 2016

Dr. Vrushali S. Kashikar
Dr. Amol A. Kulkarni
Dr. Indrajeet D. Gonjari

Acknowledgement

This book is a positive outcome of **teaching and learning experiences** with the students of Third year B. Pharm course at Modern College of Pharmacy (L), Moshi, Pune for last 10-12 years.

Our deepest gratitude goes to our **Family**, *Parents*, *Brother and our Daughter and Son* for their *full-hearted co-operation, love and moral support made us to complete this book successfully.*

One can never consent to creep when one feels an impulse to soar. We will always be thankful to **The Almighty of GOD** for giving us the strength, will and wisdom to compile this book.

We express our profound and deep sense of gratitude towards Mr. S.B. Gokhale for motivation and support.

We extend our sincere thanks to Mr. Dineshbhai Furia, Mr. Jignesh Furia and all staff members of Nirali Prakashan, for completion of this book.

December 2016

Dr. Vrushali S. Kashikar
Dr. Amol A. Kulkarni
Dr. Indrajeet D. Gonjari

Syllabus

Learning Objective: *On completion of following theory topics & laboratory experiments,*

learner should be able to:

1. *Explain disperse systems, its classification, theories of disperse systems, thermodynamic v/s kinetic stability considerations.*

2. *Explain suspensions, types, formulation development, manufacturing, excipients used, evaluation of suspensions etc.*

3. *Describe emulsions, their physico-chemical properties, theory of emulsification, HLB value and phase inversion temperature, Kraft point, cloud point, excipients, formulation and evaluation of emulsions; cracking, coalescence, stability and stress testing.*

4. *Explain semi-solids, anatomy and physiology of skin, selection of bases; penetration enhancers, formulation development, Percutaneous absorption, flux measurement and evaluation.*

5. *Describe layout for manufacturing of suspensions, emulsions and semi-solids as per schedule M.*

Skills:

1. *State the correct use of various equipments in Pharmaceutics laboratory relevant to suspensions, emulsions and semi-solids, prepare BMR.*

2. *Explain and carry out formulation of suspensions like Calamine lotion, Milk of Magnesia, Paracetamol Suspension, Antacid Suspension and carry out Evaluation.*

3. *Formulate emulsions: Liquid paraffin oral emulsion, Turpentine Liniment, Formulation of Emulsion with HLB Consideration and Evaluation.*

4. *Describe use of ingredients in formulation and category of formulation.*

5. *Prepare semisolids: Pain balm, Antifungal ointment/cream, Medicated Gel, Antiacne preparation, Non-staining Iodine ointment with Methyl Salicylate and evaluation.*

6. *Prepare the labels so as to suit the regulatory requirements.*

1. **Disperse systems:** Free energy consideration, thermodynamic v/s kinetic stability. DLVO theory, Classification of disperse system **(4 Hrs.)**

2. **Suspensions:** Flocculated and Deflocculated system. Stoke's law. Formulation development, manufacturing, Excipients used in suspensions: Suspending agents, wetting agents, dispersants, deflocculating and flocculating agents, Structured vehicle, preservatives, color, flavor. Formulation of suspensions: Low solid content, high solid content, antacid suspension, suspensions for reconstitution. Evaluation of suspensions: Rheology, Particle size, volume of sedimentation and degree of sedimentation, particle charges and caking in suspensions, importance of changes in solubility because of changes in particle size, polymorphic form temperature, labeling of suspensions. **(12 Hrs.)**

3. **Emulsions:** Physicochemical principles, theory of emulsification, energy barriers to coalescence. Film barriers, steric stabilization. Stability of emulsions: Creaming, coalescence, cracking, HLB value and phase inversion temperature, kraft point, cloud point. Excipients used in emulsions: Emulsifier and choice of emulsifier, vehicles, preservatives, antioxidants, color, flavour. Formulation of emulsions, Multiple emulsions, Microemulsions. Evaluation of emulsion, Emulsion stability, Stress testing. Evaluation: Phase separation, pH, globule size, viscosity, redispersibility. **(12 Hrs.)**

4. **Semisolid Dosage Forms:** Anatomy and physiology of skin (Introduction) Types: ointment, cream, paste and gels. Formulation development and manufacturing: Semisolid bases and additives, special reference to penetration enhancers, Selection criteria of bases. Percutaneous absorption: Flux and its measurement, factors affecting drugs. Properties, vehicle related and patient related Evaluation parameters: globule particle size, pH, spreadability, permeation, drug release, viscosity, drug content, extrudability, skin irritation test, **(12 Hrs.)**

5. **Manufacturing Equipments:** Suspension, emulsion and semisolids, Layout and designing of manufacturing facility for suspension, emulsion and semisolids as per schedule M.

Contents

1. DISPERSE SYSTEMS   **1.1 – 1.5**

  1.1   Interfacial properties of Suspended Particles   1.1
      1.1.1 Free Energy Consideration   1.1
  1.2   Stability of Suspension/Electrical Properties of Interfaces   1.2
      1.2.1 A DLVO Theory   1.2
  1.3   Fundamental Properties of Dispersed Systems.   1.4
      1.3.1 Particle Properties   1.4
      1.3.2 Surface Properties and Interfacial Phenomena   1.5

2. SUSPENSION   **2.1 – 2.21**

  2.1   Introduction   2.1
  2.2   Flocculated and Deflocculated System – Stoke's Law   2.3
      2.2.1 Theory of Sedimentation   2.3
      2.2.2 Sedimentation of Flocculated Particles   2.4
      2.2.3 Sedimentation Parameters   2.4
      2.2.4 Redispersability   2.6
  2.3   Electrokinetic Properties   2.7
      2.3.1 Nernst Potential   2.7
  2.4   Formulation Development of Suspension   2.8
      2.4.1 Dispersion Method   2.8
  2.5   Equipments used for Milling of Solid Particle before Dispersion into Suspension   2.8
      2.5.1 Fluid Energy Mill   2.8
      2.5.2 Ball Mill   2.9
      2.5.3 Micronizer   2.10
      2.5.4 Edge Runner Mill   2.11
      2.5.5 Hammer Mill   2.12
      2.5.6 Roller Mill   2.13
  2.6   Excipients used in Suspensions   2.14
  2.7   Controlled Flocculation   2.16
      2.7.1 Flocculation in Structured Vehicle   2.17
  2.8   Crystal Growth and Polymorphism   2.19
  2.9   Dry Suspension for Reconstitution   2.20
  2.10 Packaging and Storage of Suspensions   2.21

3. EMULSION   **3.1 – 3.38**

  3.1   Introduction   3.1
  3.2   Physicochemical Principles   3.2
  3.3   Physical Parameters   3.3
  3.4   Theory of Emulsion Stabilization   3.4
  3.5   Hydrophilic Lipophilic Balance   3.7
  3.6   Ostwald Ripening   3.8
  3.7   Kraft Point and Cloud Point   3.8
  3.8   Phase Viscosity   3.9

3.9	Energy Barrier	3.9
3.10	Physical Stability of Emulsions	3.11
3.11	Formulation Additives	3.14
3.12	Techniques of Emulsification	3.19
3.13	Methods for Emulsion Formulation	3.20
3.14	Equipments for Emulsion Manufacturing	3.21
	3.14.1 Agitators	3.21
	3.14.2 Mechanical Mixers	3.21
	3.14.3 Colloid Mills	3.22
	3.14.4 Homogenizers	3.23
	3.14.5 Ultrasonic Devices	3.25
3.15	Multiple Emulsion	3.25
3.16	Microemulsion	3.27
3.17	Assessment of Emulsion – Shelf Life	3.30
3.18	Characterization of Dispersed System (Suspension and Emulsion)	3.35
4.	**SEMISOLID DOSAGE FORMS**	**4.1 – 4.34**
4.1	Introduction	4.1
4.2	Anatomy and Physiology of the Skin	4.2
	4.2.1 Layers of the Skin	4.2
	4.2.2 Functions of the Skin	4.4
4.3	Ideal Properties of Semisolid Dosage Forms	4.5
	4.3.1 Ideal Molecular Properties for Drug Penetration	4.6
4.4	Types of Conventional Semisolid Dosage Forms	4.6
4.5	Percutaneous Absorption	4.7
	4.5.1 Factors Affecting Percutaneous Absorption	4.8
4.6	Process Parameters and Formulation	4.10
	4.6.1 Ointment Bases	4.10
	4.6.2 Penetration Enhancers	4.14
4.7	Method of Preparation of Ointments (Small Scale)	4.19
4.8	Manufacturing of Semisolids	4.20
4.9	Gels	4.24
4.10	Gelling Agents	4.25
4.11	Preparation and Packaging	4.28
4.12	Evaluation of Semisolids	4.29
	4.12.1 Particle Size Distribution and Particulate Nature of Semisolid Suspension	4.30
	4.12.2 Skin Irritation Tests	4.31
	4.12.3 Measurement of Skin Absorption	4.33
4.13	Labelling and Plant Layout	4.33
5.	**MANUFACTURING EQUIPMENTS**	**5.1 – 5.1**
*	**University Question Papers**	**P.1 – P.4**
*	**Bibliography**	**B.1 – B.1**
*	**Index**	**I.1 – I.3**

CHAPTER 1

DISPERSE SYSTEMS

Contents

1.1 Interfacial Properties of Suspended Particles
1.1.1 Free Energy Consideration
1.2 Stability of Suspension/Electrical Properties of Interfaces
1.2.1 A DLVO Theory
1.3 Fundamental Properties of Dispersed Systems.
1.3.1 Particle Properties
1.3.2 Surface Properties and Interfacial Phenomena

Disperse systems consist of particulate matter (dispersed phase) and continuous medium (dispersion medium).

1.1 INTERFACIAL PROPERTIES OF SUSPENDED PARTICLES

1.1.1 Free Energy Consideration

The comminution results in the large surface area of the particles and is associated with a surface free energy that makes the system thermodynamically unstable, which means the particles are highly energetic and tend to regroup in order to decrease the total surface area and to reduce the surface free energy. The particles in a liquid suspension therefore tend to flocculate, form light, fluffy coaglomerates which held together by weak Van der Waals forces. Under certain conditions in compacted cake, the particles may adhere by stronger forces termed as aggregates. Caking often occurs by the growth and fusing together of crystals in the precipitates to produce a solid aggregate. The formation of agglomerate, either floccules or aggregates, is indication of the tendency of systems to reach a more thermodynamically stable state. An increase in the work (W) or surface free energy (ΔG), caused by the comminution and consequently increasing the total surface area, ΔA, is given by,

$$\Delta G = \gamma_{SL} \cdot \Delta A$$

where, γ_{SL} is the interfacial tension between the liquid medium and the solid particles.

To approach a stable state, the system tends to reduce the surface free energy; equilibrium is reached when $\Delta G = 0$. This condition can be accomplished, by a reduction of interfacial tension or it can be approached by a decrease of the interfacial area. The later possibility leading to flocculation or aggregation, can be desirable or undesirable in pharmaceutical suspension. The interfacial tension can be reduced by the addition of a surfactant but cannot ordinarily be made equal to zero. A suspension of insoluble particles usually possesses a finite positive interfacial tension and the particles tend to flocculate.

1.2 STABILITY OF SUSPENSION / ELECTRICAL PROPERTIES OF INTERFACES

1.2.1 A DLVO (Derjaguin, Landau or Verwey and Overbeek) Theory

Most insoluble materials, solids or liquids, when dispersed within an aqueous medium develop a surface charge. The development of charges is due to the ionization of one of the functional groups present at the surface and may be due to adsorption or desorption of protons. When a charged particle is dispersed within a continuous medium containing dissolved ions either cations or anions, interaction amongst charges takes place. A DLVO theory gives focus on the energy of interaction between dispersed particles. Thus correlates the stability of dispersed system to the electrolyte/ionic contents in the continuous phase. The theory also elaborates the factors responsible for controlling the rate at which particles in the dispersed system coming into contact or aggregate. The process of aggregation accelerates sedimentation of dispersed phase particle and thus affects redispersability.

The presence of magnitude or absence of charge on a colloidal particle is an important factor in the stability of colloidal system. A lyophobic sol is said to be thermodynamically unstable and can be stabilized by developing electrical charges on the surface. As like charges produce repulsion and prevents coagulation but if the particles are allowed to aggregate cause reduction in total surface area and rapid rate of settling owing to increased size. Hence addition of small amount of electrolyte tends to stabilize the system by imparting a charge to the particles. Addition of electrolyte in excess that is necessary for maximum adsorption on the particles sometimes results in the accumulation of opposite ions and reduce zeta potential below its critical value.

A DLVO theory describes the stability of lyophobic colloids. According to this theory, the forces on the colloidal particles in dispersion are due to electrostatic repulsion and London types Van der Waal attraction. This theory elaborates a typical potential energy curve for the interaction of two charged particles as a function of inter-particle distance. In a typical potential energy curve, the attractive energy curve is V_A the repulsive energy curve V_R and the net composite or the total potential energy curve V_T. The total energy of interaction V_T between two particles is defined as sum of attraction (V_A) and repulsion (V_T) energies. From these curves it is evident that the attractive potential is predominant at short distances and net interaction is attraction in the deep potential energy minimum V_P. While at greater distances, electrostatic repulsion energy falls of more rapidly with increase in distance than the *Van der Waal* attraction energy. Thus, the net interaction is the attraction shallow secondary minimum V_S. At intermediate distances the electrostatic repulsion predominates and net interaction is with the maximum potential V_{max}. This potential energy barrier must be surmounted if the particles are to approach each other sufficiently closely to fall into deep primary energy minimum causing irreversible coagulation. To gain information about the stability of the dispersed system, it is important to compare the total energy of particles with the kinetic energy of particles, KT (Boltzman Constant).

According to DLVO theory, dispersed system becomes unstable whenever their kinetic energy is sufficient to overcome the potential energy barrier V_{max}. Thus the instability of dispersed system increases when decrease in the height/magnitude of energy barrier i.e. V_{max}. The reduction of V_{max} results from the addition of substances that neutralize the surface particle charge or cause the loss of hydration layer, compress the electrical double layer and/or cause adsorbed species to desorb from the particle surface.

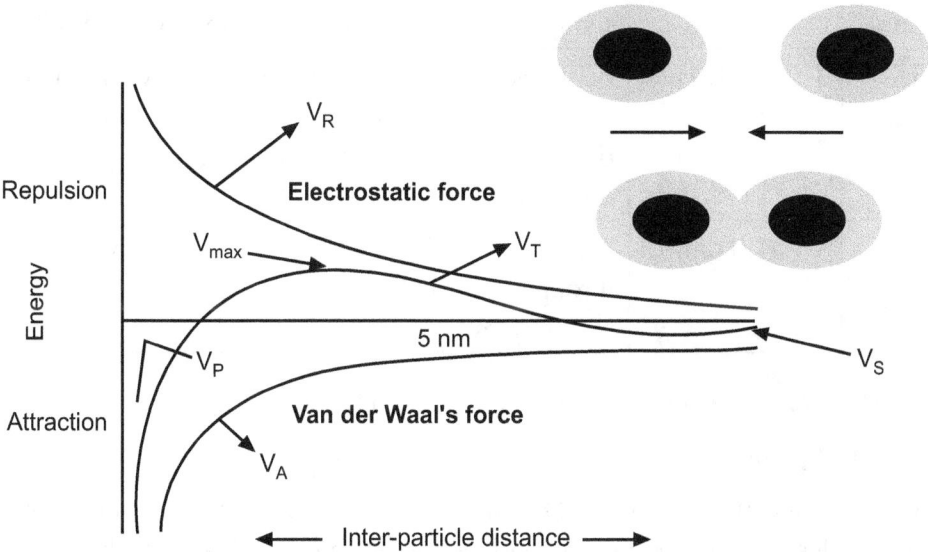

Fig. 1.1: Forces on the Colloidal Particles in Dispersion

The potential gradient strongly depends on the concentration and charge of electrolyte and also degree of hydration. As the valency increases, concentration of electrolyte requirement to cause flocculation decreases. According to Schulze-Hardy rule, fewer Al^{+3} ions are required to flocculate suspension than Na^+. The quantity of electrolyte required to cause flocculation decreases by a factor of 10 when a monovalent electrolyte is replaced by divalent electrolyte.

Table 1.1 (a) : Classification of Dispersed Systems Based on the Physical State of the Dispersed Phase/Medium

Dispersed Phase	Dispersion Medium		
	Solid	**Liquid**	**Gas**
Solid	Solid suspension	Suspension	Solid aerosol
Liquid	Solid emulsion	Emulsion	Liquid aerosol
Gas	Solid foam, Foamed plastics, Pumice	Foam, Effervescent salts in water, Carbonated beverages	None

Table 1.1 (b) : Classification of Dispersed Systems Based on Particle Size of the Dispersed Phase

Category	Range of Particle Size	Characteristics of System
Molecular dispersion	<1.0 nm	Particles invisible by electron microscopy; pass through semipermeable membranes; generally rapid diffusion.
Colloidal dispersion	1.0 nm-1.0 μm	Particles are not resolved by ordinary microscope but visible by electron microscopy; pass through filter paper but no semipermeable membranes; generally slow diffusion.
Coarse dispersion	>1.0 μm	Particles visible by ordinary microscopy; do not pass through normal filter paper or semipermeable membranes.

1.3 FUNDAMENTAL PROPERTIES OF DISPERSED SYSTEMS

1.3.1 Particle Properties

The most significant characteristics of dispersed systems are the size and shape of the dispersed particles. Both properties depend largely on the chemical and physical nature of the dispersed phase and on the method used to prepare the systems. The mean particle diameter as well as the particle size distribution of the dispersed phase has a profound effect on the properties of dosage forms, such as product appearance, settling rate, drug solubility, resuspendability, and stability.

(i) Particle Shape

Most common shapes found with pharmaceutical solids are spheres, cylinders, rods, needles and various crystalline shapes. Emulsification processes produce spherical droplets of the internal phase to minimize the interfacial area between the two phases. The deviation from sphericity characterizes the particle shape. The surface and volume are important properties affected by the overall shape of a particle.

The information on particle shape is necessary for the understanding of the behavior of suspended particles that may have an impact on the packing of sediment (packing density and settling characteristics) and thus the resuspendability and stability of the product.

Packing density is defined as the weight-to-volume ratio of the sediment at equilibrium. A wide particle size distribution often results in a high density suspension, whereas widely differing particle shapes like plates, needles, filaments, prisms etc. often result in low density. The viscosity of colloidal dispersions is affected by the shape of dispersed phases. The properties such as flow, sedimentation and osmotic pressure are also affected by the changes in particle shape of colloids.

(ii) Particle Size and Size Distribution

The particle size data can be presented by graphical and digital methods. The number/ weight of particles falls within a certain size range if plotted, against the size range/mean particle size, histogram or a frequency distribution curve can be obtained. Alternatively, the cumulative percentage over/under a particular size can be plotted against a particular size. This results in a typical sigmoid curve called a cumulative frequency plot. From these data, the mean particle size, standard deviation and the extent of polydispersity can be determined. Particle weight data is more significant in sedimentation studies, whereas number data is significant in dissolution study. A counting technique such as microscopy, while values based on weight are usually obtained by sedimentation or sieving methods can be used.

1.3.2 Surface Properties and Interfacial Phenomena

The surface free energy increases as the particle size is reduced which results in increase in specific surface area. An interfacial phenomenon deals with the presence of an electrical charge on the particle surface.

CHAPTER 2

SUSPENSION

Contents

2.1 Introduction
2.2 Flocculated and Deflocculated System – Stoke's Law
    2.2.1 Theory of Sedimentation
    2.2.2 Sedimentation of Flocculated Particles
    2.2.3 Sedimentation Parameters
    2.2.4 Redispersability
2.3 Electrokinetic Properties
    2.3.1 Nernst Potential
2.4 Formulation and Development of Suspension
    2.4.1 Dispersion Method
2.5 Equipments used for Milling of Solid Particle before Dispersion into Suspension
    2.5.1 Fluid Energy Mill
    2.5.2 Ball Mill
    2.5.3 Micronizer
    2.5.4 Edge Runner Mill
    2.5.5 Hammer Mill
    2.5.6 Roller Mill
2.6 Excipients used in Suspensions
2.7 Controlled Flocculation
    2.7.1 Flocculation in Structured Vehicle
2.8 Crystal Growth and Polymorphism
2.9 Dry Suspension for Reconstitution
2.10 Packaging and Storage of Suspension

2.1 INTRODUCTION

Pharmaceutical suspensions are uniform dispersions of solid drug particles in a vehicle in which the drug has minimum solubility.

Pharmaceutical Applications of Suspensions

• Insoluble drug or poorly soluble drugs which are required to be given orally in liquid dosage forms (children, elderly patients having difficulty in swallowing solid dosage forms).

- To overcome the instability of certain drug in aqueous solution.
- Reduce the contact time between solid drug particles and dispersion media that increase the stability of drug like Ampicillin by making as a reconstituted powder.
- A drug that is degraded in the presence of water can be suspended in non-aqueous vehicles.
- Taste masking-Example: Paracetamol suspension (more palatable).
- Some materials are needed to be present as finely divided forms to increase the surface area. Example: Magnesium carbonate and magnesium trisilicate are used to adsorb some toxins.
- Suspension can be used for topical application and parenteral administration.
- Vaccines-Example: Diphtheria and Tetanus vaccines.

At present, many drug formulations are available as suspensions. Some therapeutic classes of drug formulations are as mentioned below:

- Antacid oral suspension
- Antibacterial oral suspension
- Dry powders for oral suspension (antibiotic)
- Analgesic oral suspension
- Anthelmentic oral suspension
- Anticonvulsant oral suspension
- Antifungal oral suspension

Fig. 2.1: Marketed Preparations

A well-formulated suspension should have the following properties:

1. The dispersed particles should not settle readily and should be redispersed immediately on shacking. Ideally, the particles in a suspension should not sediment at any time during the storage period. Since one cannot completely avoid the

sedimentation of particles, it is desirable that the particles should settle slowly. The easy redispersion of sediment is important for the dose uniformity.

2. The particle should not form a hard cake on settling.

3. The viscosity should be such that the preparation can be easily poured. A highly viscous suspension would make difficulty in pouring.

4. It should be chemically and physically stable.

5. It should be palatable.

6. It should be free from grittiness (external use).

2.2 FLOCCULATED AND DEFLOCCULATED SYSTEM - STOKES'S LAW

2.2.1 Theory of Sedimentation

The velocity of sedimentation is expressed by Stokes's law,

$$V = d^2 (\rho_2 - \rho_1) g / 18\eta$$

where, V is the terminal velocity in cm/sec, d is the diameter of the particle in cm, ρ_2 and ρ_1 are the densities of the dispersed phase and dispersion medium, respectively, g is the acceleration due to gravity and η is the viscosity of the dispersion medium in poise. Particle diameter is 1 to 50 micrometer for most good pharmaceutical suspensions.

Dilute pharmaceutical suspensions (containing less than two grams of solids per 100 ml of liquid) comply roughly to these conditions. In dilute suspension, the particles do not interfere with one another during sedimentation and free settling occurs. Most pharmaceutical suspensions containing dispersed particles in concentration of 5 percent, 10 percent or higher, the particles exhibit hindered settling. The particles interfere with one another as they fall and Stokes's law no longer applies.

In concentrated suspensions, physical stability can be determined by diluting the suspension so that it contain about 0.5 percent to 2.0 percent w/v of dispersed phase. This is not always recommended, however, because the stability picture obtained is not necessarily that of the original suspension. The addition of diluents may affect the degree of flocculation (or deflocculation) of the system, thereby considerably changing the particle size distribution.

One of the proposed modifications of Stokes' equation to estimate the nonuniformity in particles shape and size invariably occurred in real systems is,

$$v' = v\epsilon^\eta$$

where v' is the rate of fall at the interface in cm/sec and v is the velocity of sedimentation according to Stokes's law. The term ϵ represent the initial porosity of the system, that is, the initial volume fraction of the uniformly mixed suspension, which varies from zero to unity. The exponent η is a measure of the "hindering" of the system. It is a constant for each system.

As given in Stoke's law, the reduction in the particle size is useful for the stability of the suspension because the rate of sedimentation decreases as the particles are decreased in size. However excessive reduction in particle size should be avoided since fine particles have a tendency to form a compact cake. The particle shape of the suspensoid can also affect caking and product stability. Example, symmetrical barrel shaped particles of calcium carbonate produce more stable suspension than did the asymmetrical needle shaped particles.

The solid content of a suspension may vary considerably depending on the dose of a drug, the volume of the product and the ability of the dispersion medium to support the concentration of drug.

2.2.2 Sedimentation of Flocculated Particles

In flocculated system, the flocs tend to fall together, producing a distinct boundary between the sediment and the supernatant liquid. The liquid above the sediment is clear because even the small particles present in the systems are associated with the flocs. This is not the case in deflocculated suspension where the larger particles settle more rapidly than the smaller particles. No clear boundary is formed (unless only one size of particle is present) and the supernatant remains cloudy for a considerably extended time period. The clear or turbid supernatant liquid during the initial phases of settling is an identification of whether the system is flocculated or deflocculated, respectively. The initial rate of settling of flocculated particles is determined by the floc size and the porosity of the aggregated mass. Subsequently, the rate depends on compaction and rearrangement process within the sediment. The term *subsidence* is sometimes used to describe settling in flocculated systems.

2.2.3 Sedimentation Parameters

The two most important parameters that are elaborated from sedimentation (subsidence) studies are sedimentation volume, V, or height, H and the degree of flocculation.

The sedimentation volume F, is defined as the ratio of the final/ultimate volume of the sediment (V_u) to the original volume of the suspension (V_o) before settling. Thus, $F = \dfrac{V_u}{V_o}$.

$$F = \frac{V_u}{V_o}$$

The values for sedimentation volume can range from less than 1 to greater than 1. Normally it is less than 1. Where, the ultimate volume of sediment is smaller than the original volume of suspension then F = 0.5. If the volume of sediment in a flocculated suspension equals the original volume of suspension, then F = 1. Such a product is said to be in "flocculation equilibrium" and shows no clear supernatant on standing. It is therefore pharmaceutically acceptable. It is possible for F to have values greater than 1, thus the final volume of sediment is greater than the original volume of suspension. Here the network of flocs formed in the suspension are so loose and fluffy that they occupy more volume than the original volume of suspension, F = 1.5.

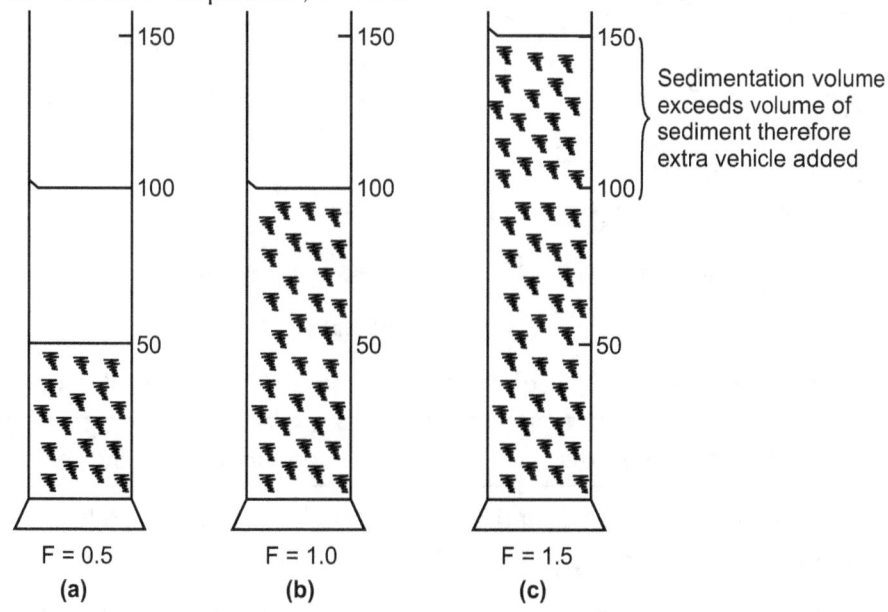

Fig. 2.2 : Sedimentation Volume

The sedimentation volume gives only qualitative account of flocculation. A more useful parameter for flocculation is β, the degree of flocculation. If we consider a suspension is completely deflocculated then ultimate volume of the sediment will be relatively small. Consider this volume as V_∞ then,

$$F_\infty = \frac{V_\infty}{V_o}$$

where F_∞ is the sedimentation volume of the deflocculated or peptized suspension. The degree of flocculation, β, is therefore defined as the ratio of F to F_∞.

$$\beta = \frac{F}{F_\infty}$$

$$= \frac{V_u / V_o}{V_\infty / V_o}$$

$$= \frac{V_u}{V_\infty}$$

$$= \frac{\text{Ultimate sediment volume of the flocculated suspension}}{\text{Ultimate sediment volume of the deflocculated suspension}}$$

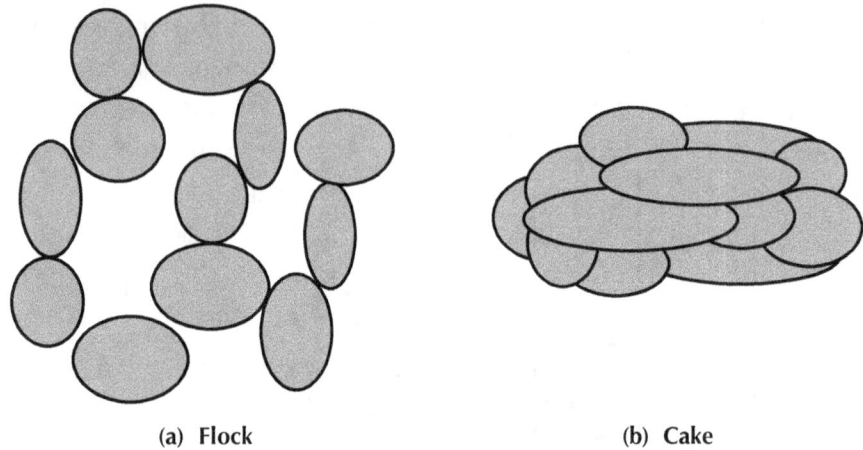

(a) Flock   (b) Cake

Fig. 2.3: Flock and Cake

Table 2.1 : Difference Between Flocculated Suspension and Non-Flocculated Suspension

Flocculated Suspension	Non-Flocculated Suspension
1. Particles form loose aggregates and form a network like structure.	1. Particles exist as separate entities.
2. Rate of sedimentation is high.	2. Rate of sedimentation is slow.
3. Sediment is rapidly formed.	3. Sediment is slowly formed.
4. Sediment is loosely packed and does not form a hard cake.	4. Sediment is very closely packed and a hard cake is formed.
5. Sediment is easy to redisperse.	5. Sediment is difficult to redisperse.
6. Suspension is not pleasing in appearance.	6. Suspension is pleasing in appearance.
7. The floccules stick to the sides of the bottle.	7. They do not stick to the sides of the bottle.

2.2.4 Redispersibility

If a pharmaceutical suspension settles during storage, then it should be readily redispersed.

The amount of shaking required should be minimal. The test for redispersibility involves the use of measuring cylinder of 100 ml capacity containing a test suspension. After prescribed period of storage and subsequent sediment, the cylinder is rotated through 360° at 20 rpm. The end point of the test is considered when no more sediment is observed at the base of the cylinder.

2.3 ELECTROKINETIC PROPERTIES

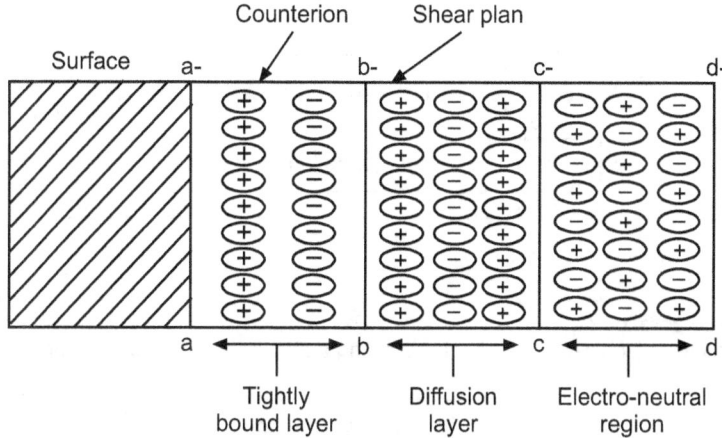

Fig. 2.4: Electrical Double Layer

In Fig. 2.4, the particle is positively charged and the anions present in the surrounding vehicle are attracted to the positively charged particle by electric forces that also serve to repel the approach of any cations. The ions that gave the particle its charge are called potential-determining ions. Immediately adjacent to the surface of the particle is a layer of tightly bound solvent molecules, together with some oppositely charged ions. These ions which are oppositely charged to the potential-determining ions are called counterions or gegenions. These two layers of ions at the interface constitute a double layer of electric charge. The intensity of the electric force decreases with distance from the surface of the particle. Thus, the distribution of ions is uniform at this region and a zone of electroneutrality is achieved.

2.3.1 Nernst and Zeta Potential

The difference in electric potential between the actual surface of the particle and the electro-neutral regions is referred to as Nernst potential. Thus, Nernst potential is controlled by the electrical potential at the surface of the particle due to the potential determining ions. Nernst potential has little effect in the formulation of stable suspension.

The potential difference between the ions in the tightly bound layer and the electro-neutral region is referred to as zeta potential and has significant effect in the formulation of stable suspension. Zeta potential governs the degree of repulsion between adjacent, similarly charged, solid dispersed particles. If the zeta potential is reduced below a critical value, the force of attraction between the particles succeeds the force of repulsion and the particles come together. This phenomenon is referred to as flocculation and the loosely packed particles are called floccule.

2.4 FORMULATION DEVELOPMENT OF SUSPENSIONS

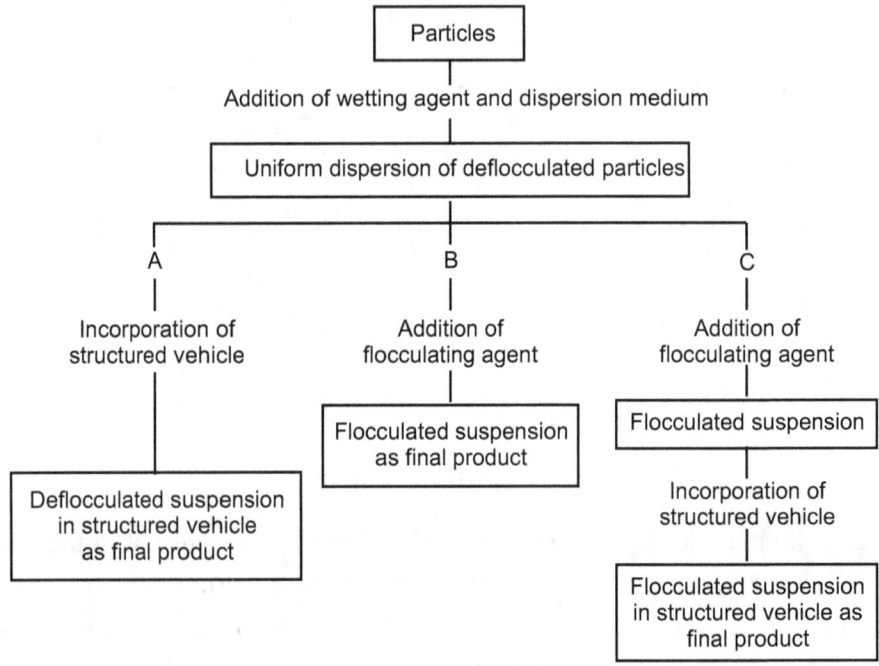

2.4.1 Dispersion Method

In these cases the powder form of the drug is directly dispersed in the liquid medium. The liquid medium should have good power of wetting the powder.

(a) Small Scale Preparation Method

A suspension is prepared on small scale by grinding or levigating the insoluble material in the mortar to a smooth paste with a vehicle containing the stabilizer and gradually adding the remaining vehicle. The slurry is transferred to a measuring cylinder; the mortar is rinsed with successive portions of the dispersion medium and finally brought to the final volume.

(b) Large Scale Preparation Method

On large scale dispersion method, the solid particles are subjected to milling before dispersion using ball, fluid energy and colloid mills.

2.5 EQUIPMENTS USED FOR MILLING OF SOLID PARTICLE BEFORE DISPERSION INTO SUSPENSION

2.5.1 The Fluid Energy Mill

Air is introduced through specially-designed fluid inlets creating sonic or supersonic air streams. The raw materials are introduced into the violent and turbulent air stream in a confined space. High velocity collisions between the raw particles lead to effective pulverization of the feed into smaller particles particularly under 10 micrometers. This method is employed when the particles are intended for parenteral and ophthalmic suspensions.

The fluid energy mill mainly used to grind the sensitive materials to the fine powder by the mechanism of impact and attrition forces applied by the air or inert gas from the nozzles present in the chamber. It works mainly on the principle of attrition and impact.

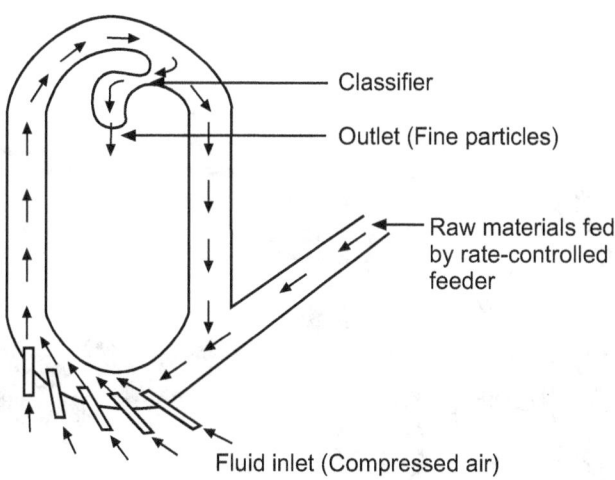

Fig. 2.5: Fluid Energy Mill/Jet Mill

The main basic parts present in the fluidized energy mill are as follows:

✓ The inlet by which the solid material is introduced into the chamber which is made up of stainless steel.

✓ The nozzles by which the air and the inert gas is introduced into the chamber at high pressure.

✓ The classifier from which the fine reduced particles are collected.

In the operation of a fluid energy mill, gas of high energy content is introduced into a pulverizing chamber. The air or inert gas is introduced with a very high pressure through the nozzles. Solids are introduced into air stream through the inlet. Due to the high degree of turbulence, impact and attritional forces occur between the particles. The fine particles are collected through a classifier. Fluid energy mill reduce the particles to 1 to 20 micron. To get a very fine powder even upto 5 micron the material is pretreated to reduce the particle size to the order of 100 meshes and then passed through fluid energy mill.

2.5.2 Ball Mill

The balls make up the grinding media and drive rollers help to rotate the milling chamber. A ball mill grinds material in a rotating cylinder with steel grinding balls, causing the balls to fall back into the cylinder and onto the material to be ground. The sample and grinding balls are placed in a grinding jar and clamped into the jar station. The milling process is initiated; the sun-wheel rotates clockwise, while the jar station rotates counter clockwise. This results in grinding balls traversing from one end of the jar to the opposing end at high speeds. The high speed impact causes a high energy collision with sample particles. In addition, the centripetal motion of the grinding action causes frictional forces that aid in fine grinding applications.

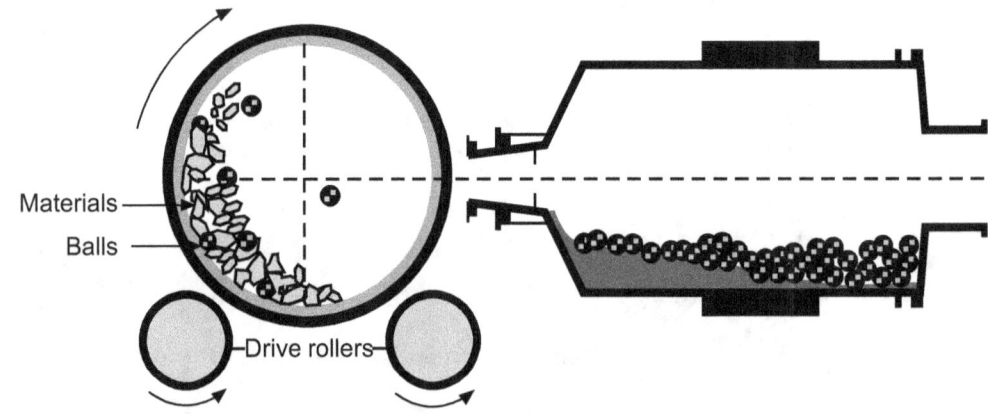

Fig. 2.6 (a): Ball Mill

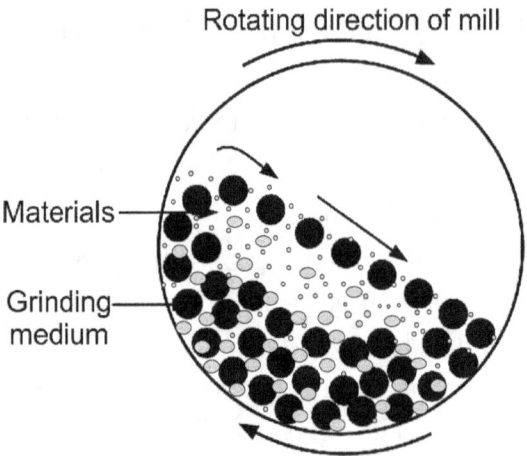

Fig. 2.6 (b) : Internal View of Ball Mill

2.5.3 Micronizer

The microparticles are forced through a minute gap in the micronizing zone. This creates conditions of high turbulence and shear, combined with compression, acceleration, pressure drop and impact, leading to the formation of a nanosuspension.

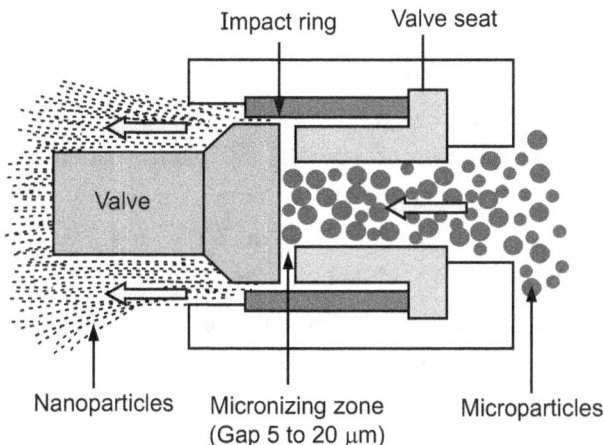

Fig. 2.7: Micronizer

2.5.4 Edge Runner Mill

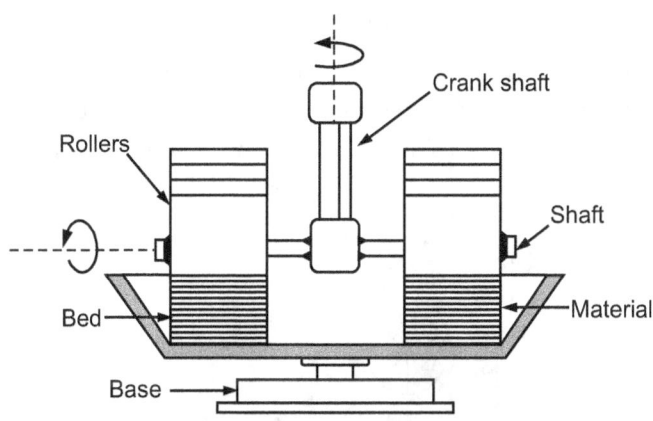

Fig. 2.8: Edge Runner Mill

Size reduction is done by crushing due to heavy weight of stones. The edge runner mill is also known as roller stone mill which crushes the materials into fine powders by the rotating stones. The edge runner mill consists of two large rotating grinding wheels turning slowly in a large bowl. An electric motor in the basement provides power for the mill. Material can be crushed in a continuous operation and the crushing is done by the heavy roller wheels or stones. The crushed powder is discharged through outlet. The edge runner mill mainly works on the attrition and impaction. It consists of two heavy rollers which are used for the grinding of the materials. It rotates mainly on central shaft. The rollers are mounted on the horizontal shaft and move around the bed. Very fine particle material can be obtained by this edge runner mill. Edge runner mill is used for grinding most of the drugs to fine powder, but it requires more floor space than the other commonly used mills. It is used to crush or grind all types of the vegetable drugs and chemicals. It is not used for sticky materials. It creates noise pollution.

2.5.5 Hammer Mill

Mill operates on the principle of impact between rapidly moving hammers mounted on a rotor. Hammer mill is a machine whose purpose is to crush aggregate material into smaller pieces. A hammer mill is a crusher that can grind, pulverize and crush a wide range of materials. Hammer mill is defined as the device or the operator which is used to crush or milling of the agglomerates or large sized particles into small sized particles with free flow properties depending upon the speed used in the mill.

Hammer mills produce a finish product size that is dependent upon,

1. Openings in perforated screens or grate bars
2. Number, size and type of hammers
3. Grinding plate setting
4. Rotor speed

Hammer mill is mainly operated at 2500 rpm or 1000 to 2500 rpm for the reduction of the large sized particles. High speed rotor uses 10000 rpm.

The material is fed at the top or the centre, thrown out centrifugally and ground around the periphery of the casing. The clearance between the housing and the hammers contributes to size reduction. The particle size of the discharged material is smaller than the screen holes.

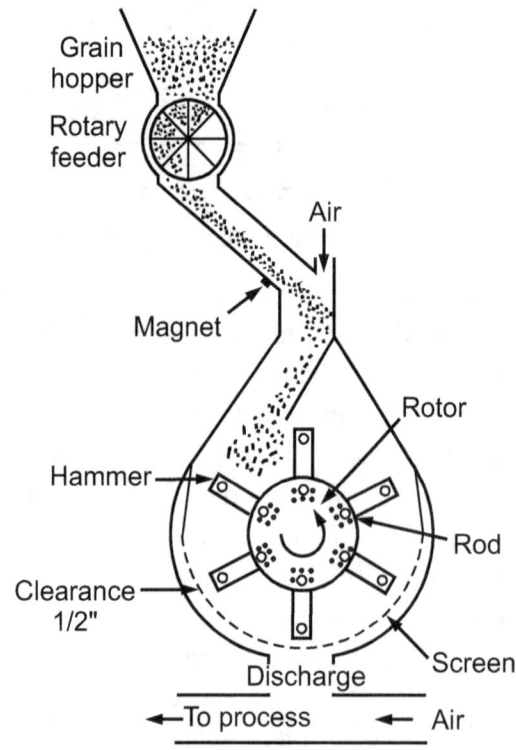

Fig. 2.9: Hammer Mill

The hammer mill consists of three basic parts as follows:
- Feed chute, which delivers the material.
- Grinding mechanism usually consisting of a rotor and stator.
- The discharging chute

A hammer mill is essentially a steel drum containing a vertical or horizontal rotating shaft or drum on which hammers are mounted. The hammers swing on the ends of the cross freely or fixed to the central rotor. The rotor rotates at a high speed inside the drum while material is fed into a feed hopper. The material is impacted by the hammer bars and expelled through screens in the drum of a selected size.

Advantages:
- Hammer mill produces ultrafine particles and yields narrow size distribution.
- It is simple to install and operate.
- The speed and screen can be rapidly changed.
- This is easy to clean and can be operated as a close system to reduce dust and explosion hazards.
- The mill efficiency and ease of manufacture, allowing easier local construction.
- Moreover, maintenance is easy and inexpensive.

2.5.6 Roller Mill

The material is crushed by application of stress through rotating heavy rollers.

The material is crushed by the application of the pressure. The mill works on the principle of compression of the material by applying the pressure on it. While working the motor drives the hanger of the grinding roller to rotate through pulley and centre bearing. The materials which are used to be crushed are fed from the hopper into the gap between the two rollers.

Due to the rotation of these rollers, the material is crushed. The gap between the rollers can be adjusted to control the degree of the size reduction. The roller mill allows crushing with a narrow particle size distribution. The narrow particle size spectrum is achieved by means of a continuous compressive shear action between two corrugated rollers with a defined roller gap.

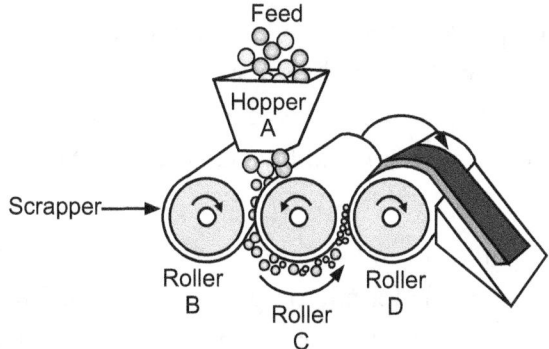

Fig. 2.10: Roller Mill

2.6 EXCIPIENTS USED IN SUSPENSIONS

(1) Suspending Agent/Surfactant

Surfactants are defined as compounds which possess in the same molecule distinct region of hydrophilic and lipophilic character. There are six functional categories for surfactant such as, cleansing agents, emulsifying agents, foam boosters, hydrotopes, solubilizing agents and suspending agents. The most useful and widely accepted classification is based on the nature of the hydrophilic head group. This approach creates four large groups of surfactant as, anionics, cationic, amphoterics and non-ionics.

The concentration of surfactants used in a formulation varies from 0.05 to 0.5 percent and depends on the surfactant type and the solid contents of the dispersion. In practice, combinations of surfactant rather than single are used to prepare and stabilize dispersed systems. The combination of a more hydrophilic surfactant with a more hydrophobic surfactant leads to the formation of the complex film at the interface. Example: Tween-Span systems.

(2) Protective Colloid and Viscosity Imparting Agents

Protective colloids can be divided as synthetic and of natural origin. Protective colloids of natural origin such as gelatin, acacia and tragacanth have been used most commonly as emulsifying agents. Amongst gelatin and albumin are preferred protective colloids for stabilizing parenteral suspension because of their biocompatibility.

Besides this naturally derived protective colloids, several synthetic, water soluble substances are widely used at appropriate concentration as mucilage substitute, suspending agent, emulsifying agent and viscosity imparting agent. Synthetic cellulose derivatives include sodium CMC, HPC, HPMC and methyl cellulose etc. Many of these are used as protective colloids at low concentration approximately less than 0.1 per cent and as viscosity builder at relatively high concentration as more than 1 per cent.

(3) pH Controlling Agents

Most dispersed systems are stable over a pH range of 4-10 but flocculate under extreme pH conditions. Many chemical buffer systems have been used in suspensions to control the pH. The optimal pH is chosen to minimize solubility of the drug, control stability of the drug and to ensure compatibility and stability of other ingredients.

(4) Preservatives

Preservatives are required in most suspensions because suspending agents and sweeteners are good growth media for microorganisms. Solvents such as alcohol, glycerine and propylene glycol are often used as preservatives at concentrations approaching 10 percent.

(5) Buffering Agents, Flavors, Colorants and Preservatives

Type	Examples
Buffers	Ammonia solution, Citric acid, Fumaric acid, Sodium citrate etc.
Flavors	Cherry, Grape, Methyl salicylate, Orange, Peppermint etc.
Colorants	D & C Red No. 33 FD & C Red No. 3 D & C Yellow No. 33 etc.
Preservatives	Butyl paraben, Methyl paraben, Propyl paraben, Sodium benzoate.

(6) Wetting of Particles

The complete dispersion of an insoluble powder in a solvent is prerequisite in the manufacturing process. It is practically difficult to disperse the powder because of an adsorbed layer of air, oil, and any other contaminants. If the powder has high density, it floats on the surface of liquid. Finely powdered substances are particularly susceptible to this effect because of entrained air, and they fail to wet even in presence of suspending medium. The wetting ability of such powders can be assessed by observing the contact angle. The contact angle is approximately 90° when the particles are floating well out of the liquid. A powder that floats low in the liquid has a lesser angle and one that sinks shows no contact angle. Powders that are not easily wetted by water such as sulfur, charcoal and magnesium stearate are said to be hydrophobic. Powders that are readily wetted by water when free of adsorbed contaminants are called hydrophilic. Example: zinc oxide, talc, magnesium carbonate etc. The most common wetting agents used are alcohol, glycerine and propylene glycol.

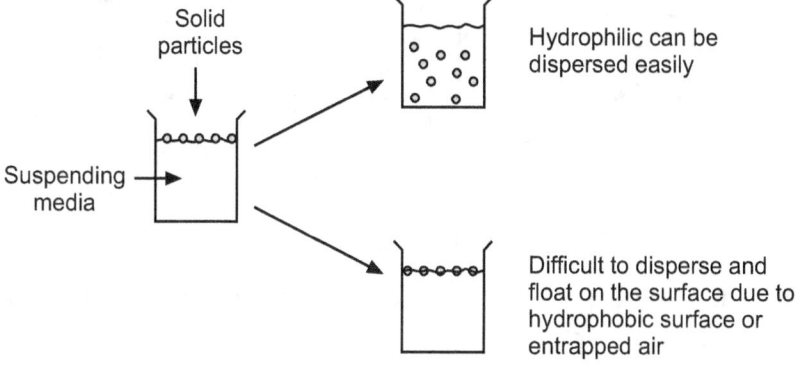

Fig. 2.11: Wetting of Particles

Surfactants are quite useful in the preparation of a suspension in reducing the interfacial tension between solid particles and a vehicle. As a result of the lowered interfacial tension, the advancing contact angle is lowered, air is displaced from the surface of particle and wetting and deflocculation are facilitated. Glycerine and similar hygroscopic substances are also valuable in levigating/lubricating the insoluble material. Glycerine flows into voids between the particles to displace the air and during mixing, coats and separates the material so that water can penetrate into and wetting initiated.

2.7 CONTROLLED FLOCCULATION

Materials used to promote flocculation in suspensions are namely electrolytes, surfactants and polymers. Electrolytes reduce electric barrier between the particles, as they cause decrease in the zeta potential and form bridge between adjacent particles so as to link them together in a loosely arranged structure. Dispersion of bismuth subnitrate in water possess a large positive charge/zeta potential. Because of the strong repulsive forces between adjacent particles, the system remains peptized or deflocculated. The addition of monobasic potassium phosphate to the dispersion of bismuth subnitrate reduces the positive zeta potential owing to the adsorption of the negatively charged phosphate anion.

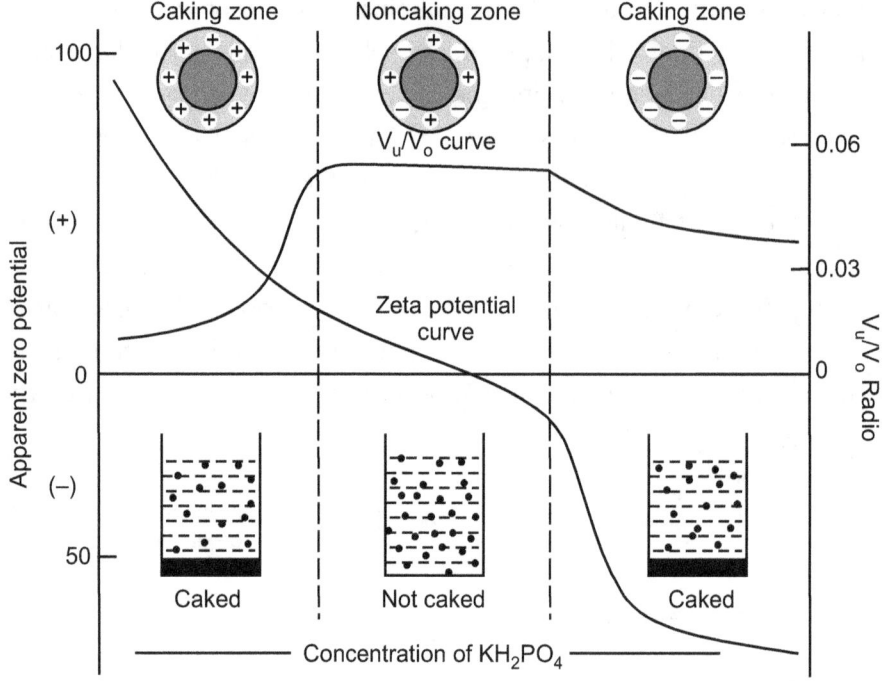

Fig. 2.12: Caking in the Suspension

With further addition of electrolytes the zeta potential eventually falls to zero and then increase in the opposite direction. At a certain positive zeta potential, maximum flocculation occurs and will persist until the zeta potential has become sufficiently negative for deflocculation to occur once again . The onset of flocculation coincides with the maximum sedimentation volume, (F) determined. F remains reasonably constant while flocculation persist and only when the zeta potential becomes sufficiently negative to effect re-peptization then start to fall. Finally, the absence of caking in the suspension correlates with the maximum sedimentation volume. At less than maximum values of F, caking becomes apparent.

A similar correlation observed when aluminium chloride was added to a suspension of sulfamerazine in water. In this system, the initial negative zeta potential reaches zero and then increases in a positive direction.

Surfactants, both ionic and nonionic, have been used to bring about flocculation of suspended particles. The concentration necessary to achieve this effect would appear to be critical because these compounds can also act as wetting and deflocculating agents to achieve dispersion. In case of ionic surfactants, the heads adsorb on the surface and tail projects outwards and forms bridge like structure between the particles. This causes flocculation.

Hydrophilic polymers also act as protective colloids. A part of these flocculating agents get adsorb on the particle surface with the remaining portion projecting out into the continuous phase, named as a bridging phenomenon.

2.7.1 Flocculation in Structured Vehicles

The controlled flocculation approach results in a stable pharmaceutical suspension, but the supernant becomes clear rapidly and the product can look unsightly if F, the sedimentation volume, is not close or equal to 1. Consequently, in practice, a suspending agent is frequently added to retard sedimentation of flocs. Such agents as carboxy methylcellulose, carbopol 934, veegum, tragacanth and bentonite have been employed, either alone or in combination.

This can lead to incompatibilities, depending on the initial particle charge and the charge carried by the flocculating agent and the suspending agent. A dispersion of positively charged particles can be prepared and then flocculated by the addition of the correct concentration of an anionic electrolyte. Physical stability can be improved by adding a small amount of one of the hydrocolloids. No physical incompatibility will be observed because the majority of hydrophilic colloids are themselves negatively charged and are thus compatible with anionic flocculating agents. If, however we flocculate a suspension of negatively charged particles with cationic electrolyte (aluminium chloride), the subsequent addition of hydrocolloid may result in an incompatible product, as evidenced by the formation of an unsightly stringy mass that has little or no suspending action and itself settles rapidly.

Hence, it becomes necessary to use a protective colloid to change the sign on the particle from negative to positive. This is achieved by the adsorption onto the particle surface of fatty acid amine (which has been checked to ensure its nontoxicity) or a material such as gelatin, which is positively charged below its isoelectric point. We can use an anionic electrolyte to produce flocs that are compatible with the negatively charged suspending agent. This approach can be used regardless of the charge on the particles.

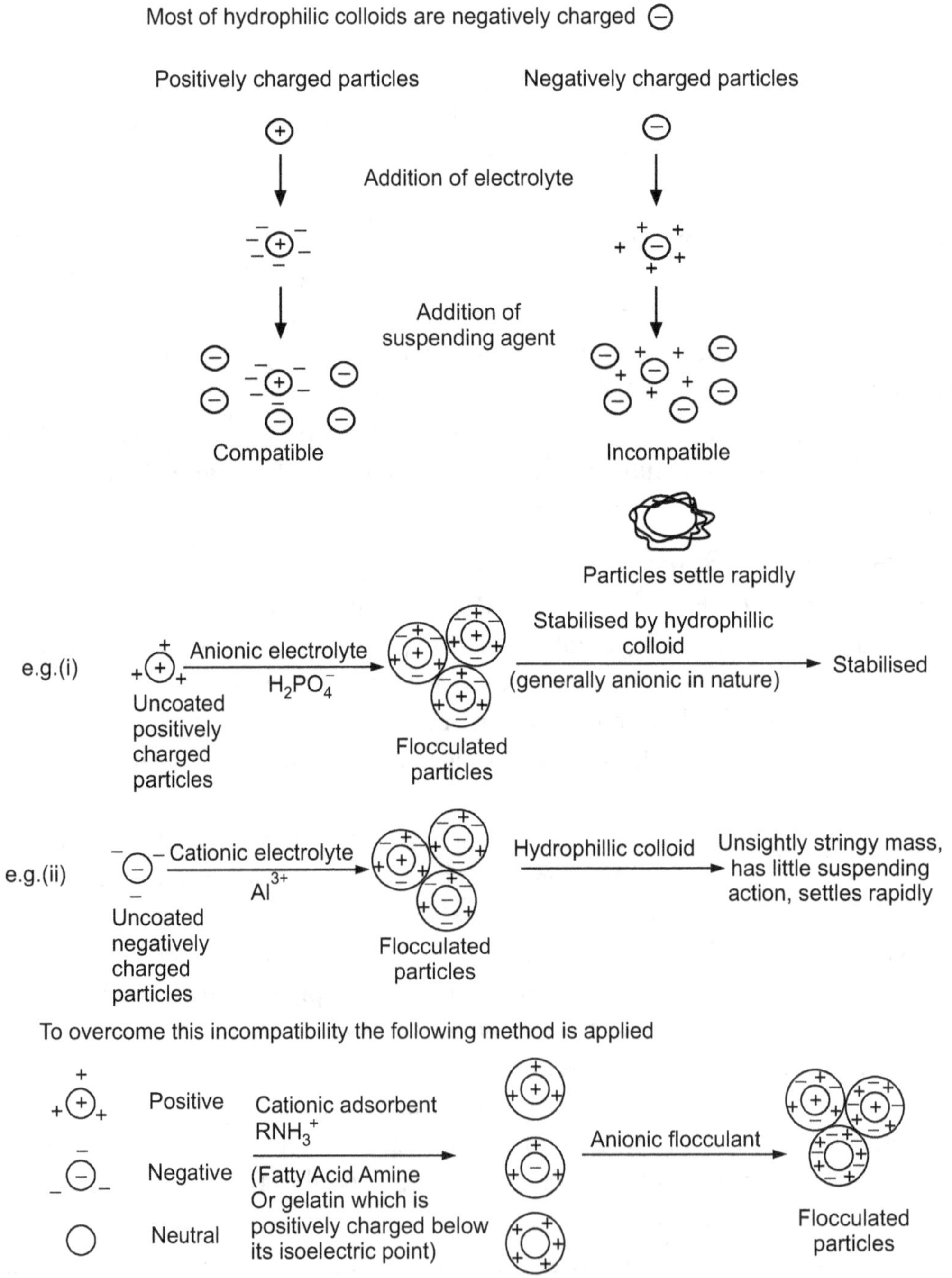

Most of hydrophilic colloids are negatively charged $\ominus$

Fig. 2.13: Flocculation in Structured Vehicles

2.8 CRYSTAL GROWTH AND POLYMORPHISM

The crystal growth in dispersed systems may take place by one or more of the following mechanism as, Oswald ripening, temperature changes and polymorphic transformation. Oswald ripening is the growth of large particles at the expense of smaller ones as a result of a difference in the solubility of particles of varying size. The surface free energy of small particles is greater than that of large particles. Small particles are reasonably more soluble than larger one. A concentration gradient results with higher drug concentration in the area of small particles and low drug concentration in the area of large particles. Thus according to Fick's law of diffusion, the dissolved particles/molecules diffuse from the environment of smaller particles. An increase in the concentration in the area of large particles leads to crystallization and particles growth. Thus, small particle becomes smaller whereas large particles become larger upon storage. Small fluctuations in temperature can accelerate this effect. Small particles dissolve to a greater extent when the temperature increases and as then recrystallize on the surface of existing larger particles as the temperature drops. Suspension becomes coarser and the mean particles size spectrum shifts to higher value.

Crystal growth due to temperature fluctuations during storage is important especially when the suspension is subjected to temperature cycling of 20°C or more. These effects depend on the magnitude of temperature change, the time interval and the effect of temperature on the drug solubility and subsequent recrystallization process.

As crystal growth generally increases with solubility, the additives that tend to increase the solubility should be added at low level. Many gums can absorb onto the surface of drug crystal and thus can be used to inhibit the crystal growth. In a dilute suspension, crystal growth increases with the degree of agitation because the mass transfer in a bulk fluid is increased. If sedimentation occurs, the local increase in particles concentration decreases the mean free diffusion path of the solute molecules and may thus promote the particle growth.

Polymorphism means the different internal crystal structure of a chemically identical compound. Drug may undergo a change from one metastable polymorphic form to a more stable polymorphic form. Also the crystal habit might change due to the degree of solvation or hydration. The formation of distinct new crystalline entities during storage is possible. Example: an originally anhydrous drug in a suspension may rapidly or slowly form a hydrate. This various form may exhibit different solubility, melting point and X ray diffraction pattern. The rate of conversion from a metastable into the stable form is an important criterion to be considered with respect to shelf life of a pharmaceutical product. Size reduction by crushing and grinding can produce particles whose different surface exhibit high or low dissolution rate. This effect can be correlated to differences in the free surface energy introduced during comminution.

To prevent crystal growth and possible changes in particle size distribution, one or more of the following procedure and techniques may be employed :

- selection of particle with a narrow size range
- selection of a more stable crystalline form of drug
- avoidance of the use of high energy milling during particle size reduction
- incorporation of a wetting agent and protective colloids
- increase of the viscosity of the vehicle to retard particle dissolution and subsequent crystal growth
- avoid temperature extreme during storage.

2.9 DRY SUSPENSIONS FOR RECONSTITUTION

Suspensions for reconstitution are dry formulations which require mixing with water prior to administration. Once reconstituted, they must conform to all of the requirements of a traditional suspension. This type of dosage form is usually used for drugs that are not stable in the presence of water but need to be dispensed in liquid form. Oral and parenteral products are included in this classification.

Formulations

In general, the number of ingredients should be kept to a minimum in order to decrease the possibility of problems. All ingredients should disperse rapidly on reconstitution; this criterion eliminates several suspending agents which require special mixing procedures for complete dispersion. Sodium carboxymethylcellulose (Na CMC), microcrystalline cellulose with Na CMC, carrageenans and xanthan gum are typical suspending agents capable of dispersing readily by shaking.

Preparation

The preparation of suspensions for reconstitution involves dry powder mixing and granulation processes. In general, the products fall into one of the three classes; powder blends, granulations or a combination of the two.

Amoxicillin Suspensions for Reconstitution

Active ingredient	Amoxicillin Trihydrate
Sweetener	Sucrose, Mannitol
Suspending agent	Xanthan gum/Cellulose/Sodium CMC
Dessicant	Silica gel
Buffer	Sodium citrate/ citric acid
Preservative	Sodium benzoate
Colorant	FD&C Red No. 3/ Red No. 28/ Red No. 40
Flavor	Artificial flavors

2.10 PACKAGING AND STORAGE OF SUSPENSIONS

1) Should be packaged in wide mouth containers having adequate air space above the liquid.

2) Should be stored in tight containers protected from freezing, excessive heat and light.

3) Label: "Shake Well Before Use" to ensure uniform distribution of solid particles and thereby uniformity in dosage.

Materials Used For Packaging

Generally glass and various grades of plastics are used in packaging of suspension. Glass generally soda lime and borosilicate glass are used in preparation of non-sterile suspensions.

Due to negative aspects of glass, use of plastic as packaging material for sterile as well as non-sterile pharmaceutical suspension increased.

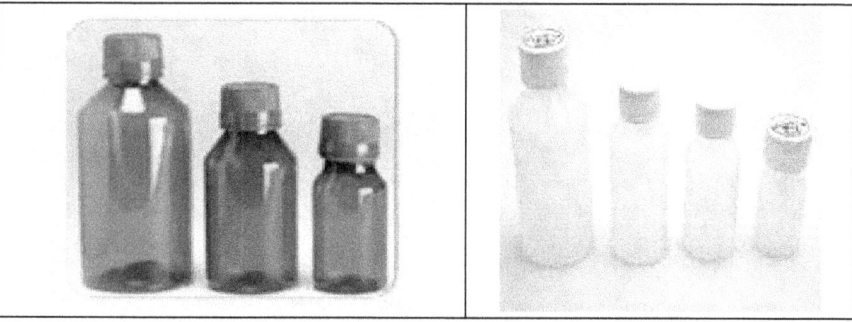

Fig. 2.14: Containers

Closure and Liners : With an exception of ampoules, all containers require elastomeric closure.

Fig. 2.15: Closure and Liners

CHAPTER 3

EMULSION

Contents

3.1   Introduction

3.2   Physicochemical Principles

3.3   Physical Parameters

3.4   Theory of Emulsion Stabilization

3.5   Hydrophilic Lipophilic Balance

3.6   Ostwald Ripening

3.7   Kraft Point and Cloud Point

3.8   Phase Viscosity

3.9   Energy Barrier

3.10 Physical Stability of Emulsions

3.11 Formulation Additives

3.12 Techniques of Emulsification

3.13 Methods for Emulsion Formulation

3.14 Equipments for Emulsion Manufacturing

    3.14.1   Agitators

    3.14.2   Mechanical Mixers

    3.14.3   Colloid mills

    3.14.4   Homogenizers

    3.14.5   Ultrasonic Devices

3.15 Multiple Emulsion

3.16 Microemulsion

3.17 Assessment of Emulsion – Shelf Life

3.18 Characterization of Dispersed System (Suspension and Emulsion)

3.1 INTRODUCTION

An emulsion is a thermodynamically unstable dispersed system consisting of at least two immiscible liquid phases, one of which is dispersed as globules in the other liquid phase. The system is stabilized by the presence of an *emulsifying agent*. Emulsified systems range from lotions of relatively low viscosity to ointments and creams, which are semisolid in nature.

The particle diameter of the dispersed phase generally extends from about 0.1 to 10 μm.

Table 3.1: Methods for the Determination of Type of Emulsion

Test	Observation	Comments
Dilution test	Emulsion can be diluted only with external phase.	Useful for liquid emulsions.
Dye test	Water soluble solid dye tints only o/w emulsion and reverse. o/w w/o	May fail if ionic emulsifiers are present.
Filter paper test/CoCl₂	Filter paper impregnated with $CoCl_2$ and dried, (blue) changes to pink when o/w emulsion is added.	May fail if emulsion is unstable or breaks in presence of electrolyte
Fluorescence test	Since oils fluoresce under UV light, o/w emulsion exhibit dot pattern, w/o emulsions fluoresce throughout.	Not always applicable
Conductivity test	Electric current is conducted by o/w emulsions, owing to presence of ionic species in water.	Fail in non-ionic o/w emulsion

3.2 PHYSICOCHEMICAL PRINCIPLES

When two immiscible liquids are mechanically agitated, both phases initially form droplets. When the agitation is stopped, the droplets undergo quick coalescence, thus the two liquids separate. The life of the droplets is eventually increased if an emulsifier is added to the two immiscible liquids. Usually, only one phase persists in droplet form for a prolonged period of time. This phase is called the internal/dispersed phase and it is surrounded by an external/continuous phase. Usually closed packed mono dispersed spherical droplets as the internal phase can occupy not more than ~74 percent of the total volume of an emulsion. However, the internal phase can exceed 74 percent if the spherical particles are not mono disperse. A further increase in the ratio of dispersed: continuous phase can be possible if the dispersed phase is assumed to consist of polyhedral/ nonspheres rather than spheres. If the oil droplets are dispersed in a continuous aqueous phase, the emulsion is termed as oil-in-water, if the oil is the continuous phase, the emulsion is of the water-in-oil type. It has been observed that o/w emulsion occasionally change into w/o emulsion and vice a versa. This change of emulsion type is called phase inversion.

The spontaneous formation of an emulsion is a relatively rare in occurrence. Instead, emulsion preparation by the dispersion method requires a sequence of processes for breaking up the internal phase into droplets and for stabilizing so formed droplets in the external phase. The complete process must be designed in such a way that these two steps are carried out before the internal phase can coalesce. Usually, the breakup of the internal phase is fairly rapid; however, it is believed that the stabilization step and the rate of coalescence are time and temperature dependent. It is therefore a requirement in the design of any emulsification process that the variable physical and chemical parameters are selected and controlled to favor emulsion formation.

3.3 PHYSICAL PARAMETERS

To reduce the internal phase into small droplets the application of energy in the form of heat, mechanical agitation, ultrasonic vibration or electricity is required. The amount of work done depends on the period of time during which energy is supplied and thus timing becomes another important physical parameter.

(i) Heat / Temperature

Vaporization is an effective way of breaking almost all the bonds between the molecules of a liquid. It is possible, therefore, to prepare emulsions by passing the vapour of a liquid into an external phase that contains suitable emulsifying agents. This process of emulsification is called the condensation method. It is relatively slow and limited to the preparation of dilute emulsions of materials having a relatively low vapour pressure. An increase in temperature decreases interfacial tension and viscosity. Usually it is assumed that emulsification is possible by an increase in temperature. At the same time an increase in temperature raises the kinetic energy of droplet and thereby facilitate droplet movements and thus chances of coalescence.

Changes in temperature alter the distribution coefficients of emulsifiers between the two phases and cause emulsifier migration, leads to phase inversion. The temperature at which the inversion occurs depends on emulsifier concentration and is called phase inversion temperature (PIT). This type of inversion can occur during the formation of emulsions, since they are generally prepared at relatively high temperatures and are then allowed to cool to room temperature. Emulsions formed by a phase inversion technique are generally considered quite stable and are believed to contain a finely dispersed internal phase. The PIT is generally considered to be the temperature at which the hydrophilic and the lipophilic properties of the emulsifier are in balance and is therefore also called the HLB temperature. Shinoda and coworkers found that many o/w emulsions stabilized with nonionic surfactants undergo a process of inversion at a critical temperature (phase inversion temperature, PIT). The PIT can be determined by following the emulsion conductivity (small amount of electrolyte is added to increase the sensitivity) as a function of temperature. The conductivity of the o/w emulsion increases with increase of temperature till the PIT is reached, above which there will be a rapid reduction in conductivity (w/o emulsion is formed). Shinoda and coworkers found that the PIT is influenced by the HLB number of the surfactant. The size of the emulsion droplets was found to depend on the temperature and HLB number of emulsifiers. Emulsions prepared at a temperature just below the PIT followed by rapid cooling generally have smaller droplet sizes.

(ii) Timing

During emulsification, droplets are formed due to agitations, however, as the process of agitation continues, facilitates droplet movements thereby the chance for collision between droplets becomes more frequent and coalescence can occur. Therefore it is suggested to avoid continuous agitation during and after formation of an emulsion. It is more accurate to use intermittent shaking. It was found that, it could possible to emulsify sixty percent by volume of benzene in one percent aqueous sodium oleate by mechanically shaking 750 times during a period of four to five minutes. The same mixture, however, could be completely emulsified with merely five handshakes in about two minutes, if the emulsion was allowed to rest for 20-30 seconds after each shake. The reasons for the observed time dependent droplet stabilization may be distribution of the emulsifier between the phases, slow formation of the film on the surface of the benzene droplets or interruption of droplet formation by continuous shaking.

(iii) Low Energy Emulsification

The principle of low energy emulsification has been established by Lin. In low energy emulsification, all of the internal phase, but only a portion of the external phase, is heated. After emulsification of the heated portions, the remaining external phase is added to the emulsion concentrate or the preformed concentrate is blended into the continuous phase. In those emulsions in which a phase inversion temperature exists, the emulsion concentrate is preferably prepared above the PIT, which results in emulsions having extremely small droplet size.

3.4 THEORY OF EMULSION STABILIZATION

Emulsifying agents assist in the formation of emulsion by three distinct mechanisms as suggested,

- Reduction of interfacial tension – thermodynamic stabilization
- Formation of rigid interfacial film – mechanical barrier to coalescence
- Formation of electrical double layer – electrical barrier approach of particles

(I) Thermodynamic Stabilization-Interfacial Films

A temporary emulsion will be formed when two immiscible liquids (Example: liquid paraffin and water) are shaken together. The subdivision of one of the phases into small droplets results in a large increase in surface area and hence the interfacial free energy of the system. The system so called thermodynamically unstable which results first in the dispersed phase being in the form of spherical droplets (the shape of minimum surface area for a given volume) and secondly in coalescence of these droplets, causing phase separation (the state of minimum surface free energy).

Surface active agents reduce interfacial tension by adsorbing at the interface of oil and water to form monomolecular film. Practically a film formed should be flexible enough so that it is capable of reforming rapidly if broken or disturbed. As well the presence of the surface charge, which will cause repulsion between adjacent particles, promote the stability to system. The work of Schulman and Cockbain in 1940 on emulsion stability showed that, the mixture of oil soluble alcohol, cholesterol and a surfactant, sodium cetyl sulphate were able to form a stable complex, condensed film at the o/w interface. This film possesses high viscosity, sufficient flexibility to permit distortion of the droplet, resisted rupture and gave an interfacial tension lower than that produced by other component alone. The stable emulsion was produced, the charge arising from the sodium cetyl sulphate contributing to the stability.

According to Schulman and Cockbain theory,

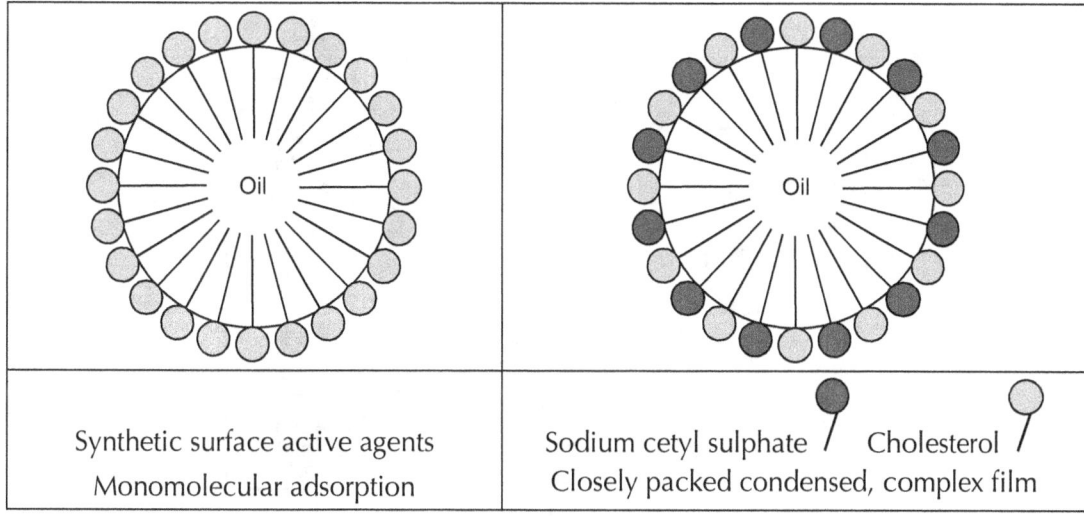

| Synthetic surface active agents
Monomolecular adsorption | Sodium cetyl sulphate / Cholesterol /
Closely packed condensed, complex film |

Fig. 3.1: Interfacial Films

(II) Mechanical Barrier to Coalescence-Hydrophillic Colloids

Hydrophillic colloids exhibit little surface activity, adsorb at the o/w interface and form multimolecular film with viscoelastic properties, resist rupture and form mechanical barrier to coalescence. Example: Protein (gelatin, casein), polysaccharides (acacia, cellulose derivatives, alginates) etc. Some of these substances possess ionizable chemical group providing electrostatic repulsion as barrier to coalescence. Example: Polysaccharide acacia consists of salts of arabic acid and proteins contain both amino and carboxylic acid group. Most cellulose derivatives are not charged and thus sterically stabilize the system. They increase viscosity of aqueous phase and prevent aggregate formation. The steric repulsive force, which depends on the concentration and degree of solvation of polymer chains, must be of sufficient magnitude to prevent close approach of the uncoated particles but low enough so that the attractive force is dominant leading to aggregation at about twice the adsorbed layer thickness.

(III) Solid Particles

Emulsions may be stabilized by finely divided solid particles if they are preferentially wetted by one phase and possess sufficient adhesion for one another so that they form a film around the dispersed droplets. Solid particles remain at the interface as long as stable contact angle θ is formed by liquid /liquid interface and solid interface. The liquid whose contact angle is less than 90° will form continuous phase. Al and Mg hydroxide, clays such as bentonite are wetted by water and therefore stabilize o/w emulsion. Example: liquid paraffin and magnesium hydroxide emulsion. Carbon black and talc are wetted by oils and stabilize w/o emulsion. Various types of film formed by the emulsifier is given below:

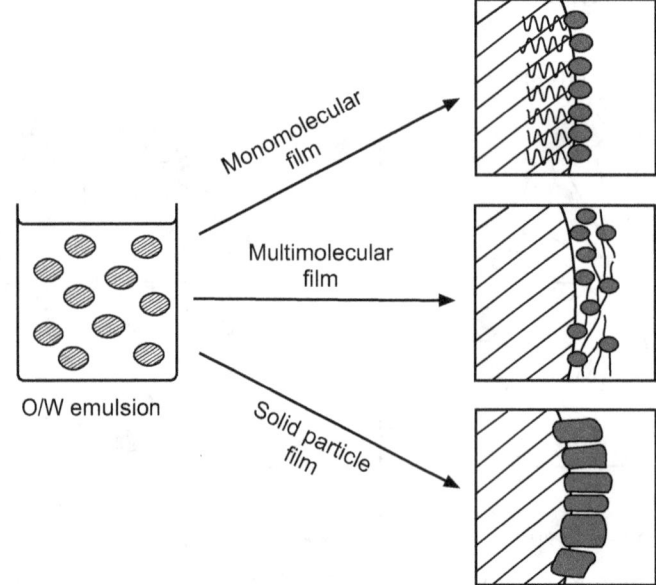

Fig. 3.2 (a) : Theory of Emulsion Stabilization

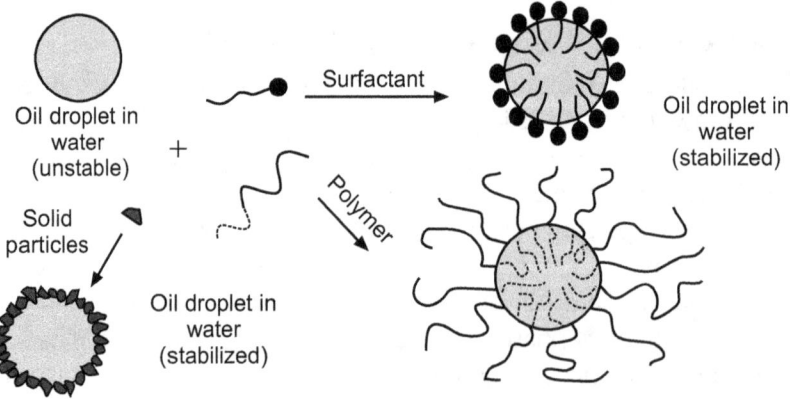

Fig. 3.2 (b) : Theory of Emulsion Stabilization

3.5 HYDROPHILIC LIPOPHILIC BALANCE (HLB)

Griffin devised an arbitrary scale of values to serve as a measure of the hydrophilic-lipophilic balance (HLB) of surface-active agents.

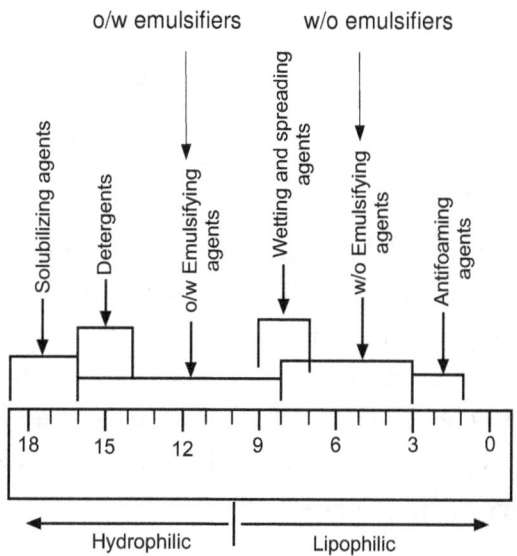

Fig. 3.3 : Griffin's HLB Scale

i) HLB value for nonionic surfactants. Example: Tweens and spans

$$HLB = (E+P)/5$$

where, E = Percent by weight of oxyethylene chain

P = percent by weight of polyhydric alcohol groups (glycerol/sorbitol) in molecule

ii) If the surfactant contains only polyethylene as hydrophobic group,

$$HLB = E/5$$

iii) General chemical formula,

$$HLB = 7 + \Sigma \text{ (hydrophilic group number)} - \Sigma \text{ (lipophilic group number)}$$

iv) HLB of polyhydric alcohol fatty acid esters such as glyceryl monostearate,

$$HLB = 20(1-S/A)$$

where, S = saponification value of ester; A = acid value of fatty acid

v) HLB of mixture of surfactants, consisting of fraction x of A and (1–x) of B is assumed to be an algebraic mean of two HLB numbers.

$$HLB_{mix} = x\ HLB_A + (1-x)\ HLB_B$$

Table 3.2 : HLB Range and its Applications

HLB Range	Application
3-6	W/O emulsifier
7-9	Wetting agent
8-18	O/W emulsifier
13-15	Detergent
15-18	Solubilizer

3.6 OSTWALD RIPENING

This results from the finite solubility of liquid phases. Liquids that are referred to as being immiscible often have mutual solubilities that are not negligible. With emulsions, which are usually polydisperse, the smaller droplets will have larger solubility when compared with the larger ones (due to curvature effects). With time, the smaller droplets disappear and their molecules diffuse to the bulk and become deposited on the larger droplets. With time, the droplet size distribution shifts to larger values.

3.7 KRAFT POINT AND CLOUD POINT

The Kraft temperature/Kraft point, or critical micelle temperature is the minimum temperature at which surfactants form micelles. It is named after German chemist Friedrich Kraft. Below the Kraft temperature, there is no value for the critical micelle concentration (CMC), micelles cannot form. The Kraft temperature is a point of phase change below which the surfactant remains in crystalline form, even in aqueous solution.

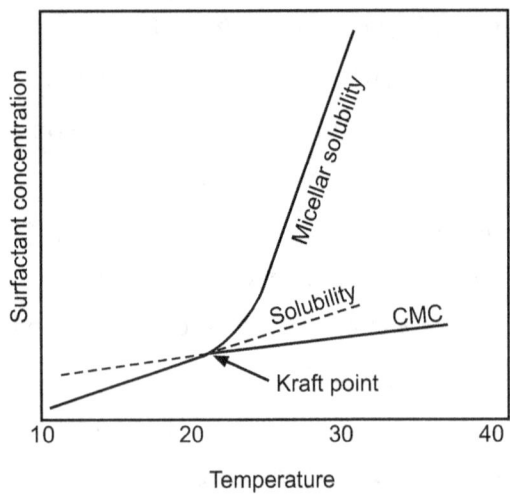

Fig. 3.4 : Kraft Point

Above the cloud point, the solution becomes cloudy or opaque due to the surfactant molecules undergoing flocculation. The solubility of ethoxylate surfactants is unusual because it decreases with increasing temperature. Ethoxylate chains tend to curl into hydrophilic coils at lower temperatures and when heated get randomized. A tube containing one percent clear solution of ethoxylate surfactants kept at room temperature if warm slowly, at a certain temperature, so called the cloud point, the tube will become cloudy. For pure ethoxylates this transition is sharp.

3.8 PHASE VISCOSITY

The emulsification process and type of emulsion formed are influenced to some extent by the viscosity of both the phases. Viscosity can be expected to affect interfacial film formation as the migration of molecule of emulsifying agent to the oil/water interface is diffusion controlled. Droplets movement prior to coalescence is also affected by the viscosity of medium in which the droplet is dispersed.

(a) Viscosity of the Continuous Phase

There is a direct relationship between viscosity of an emulsion and viscosity of continuous phase. This causes increase in density difference between the two phases and thus eventually accelerating creaming. Hydrocolloid as an emulsifying agent stabilizes emulsion by forming multimolecular layer around disperse phase globules and also by increasing the viscosity of continuous phase. If oil is continuous phase then soft, hard paraffin or some waxes will increase its viscosity.

(b) Viscosity of the Dispersed Phase

The overall effect of viscosity of dispersed phase on total emulsion viscosity is doubtful. However it is possible that a less viscous dispersed phase would deform to a greater extent than a more viscous phase. This leads to slight increase in total interfacial area and hence viscosity of the emulsion.

3.9 ENERGY BARRIER

For simple emulsion, two kinds of barriers are essential:

i)   The electrical double layer
ii) Steric repulsion from adsorbed polymer

(i) The Electrical Double Layer

An ionic surfactant adsorbed at the interface of o/w emulsion with its polar group projecting towards water. Then some counterions of the surfactants will separate out and will form diffuse cloud into continuous phase. Thus charged droplet surface shows a diffuse layer of counterions extending from it. The surface charge plus the counterions are called the electrical double layer. The potential produced by the double layer creates repulsive effect between the oil droplets and thus hinders coalescence. The repulsive electrical potential at the emulsion interface can be related to zeta potential and can be determined.

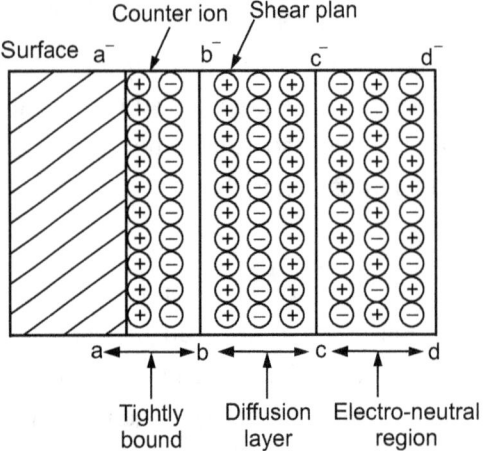

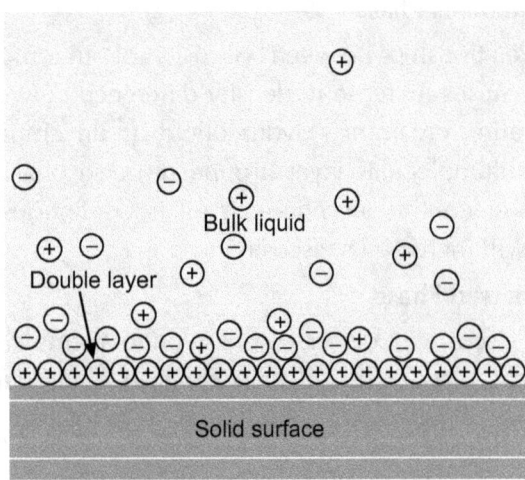

Fig. 3.5 : The Electrical Double Layer

(ii) Steric Repulsion

Use of nonionic polymeric material arises a concept of steric stabilization or protective colloid action. These material form adsorbed layer around the particles. Each adsorbed layer possess particular thickness and thus when two droplets approach each other, their aggregation to coagulated state is hindered. Repulsive force arises as the adsorbed layer fuses with each other.

As a result the particle will not usually approach one another closer than twice the thickness of the adsorbed layer. Steric repulsive forces depend on the concentration and degree of solvation of the polymer chain. Steric repulsion must be of sufficient magnitude to close approach of the uncoated particle but low enough so that the attractive force is dominant leading to aggregation at about twice the adsorbed layer thickness.

3.10 PHYSICAL STABILITY OF EMULSIONS

A stable emulsion may be defined as a system in which the globules retain their initial character and remain uniformly distributed throughout the continuous phase. The function of the emulsifying agent is to form an interfacial film around the dispersed droplets. In the light of these considerations, the instability of pharmaceutical emulsion may be classified as follows:

a) Flocculation and creaming

b) Coalescence and breaking

c) Phase inversion

d) Miscellaneous physical and chemical change

(a) Flocculation and Creaming

Flocculation should not be confused with creaming. Flocculation is due to the interaction of attractive and repulsive forces and creaming is due to density differences in the two phases. Both of these may occur. Flocculation of emulsion droplets can occur only when the mechanical or electrical barrier is sufficient to prevent droplet coalescence. In other words, flocculation differs from coalescence primarily by the fact that the interfacial film and the individual droplets remain intact. The reversibility of this type of aggregation depends on the strength of the interaction between particles as determined by the chemical nature of the emulsifier, the phase volume ratio and the concentration of dissolved substances especially electrolytes and ionic emulsifiers.

$$\text{Stoke's law equation: } \frac{dx}{dt} = \frac{d^2(\rho_2 - \rho_1)g}{18\eta}$$

Analysis of the equation shows that if the dispersed phase is denser than the continuous phase, which is generally the case in o/w emulsions, the velocity of sedimentation becomes negative, that is, an upward creaming results. If the internal phase is heavier than the external phase, the globules settle, a phenomenon noted is w/o emulsions. This effect can be referred to as creaming in a downward direction. Those factors that influence the rate of creaming are similar to those involved in sedimentation of suspended particles and are indicated by Stoke's law,

$$V = \frac{2a^2 g(\rho_2 - \rho_1)}{9\eta}$$

where, V = velocity of creaming, a = globule radius and ρ_2 and ρ_1 = densities of dispersed phase and dispersion medium.

A consideration of this equation shows that the rate of creaming will be decreased by,

(i) reduction in globule size, (ii) decrease in density difference between two phases and (iii) increase in viscosity of continuous phases.

The factor in Stoke's equation can be altered, to reduce the rate of creaming in an emulsion. The viscosity of the external phase can be increased without exceeding the limit of acceptable consistency by adding a viscosity improver or thickening agent such as methyl cellulose, tragacanth or sodium alginate. The particle size of globules can be reduced by homogenization. When the particle size is reduced to 2-5 μm in diameter, the Brownian motion at room temperature exerts sufficient influence so that the particles settle or cream more slowly than predicted by Stoke's law.

Theoretically, adjusting the external and internal phase densities to the same value should eliminate the tendency to cream. Temperature has influence on densities. Researchers have increased density of oil phase by using alpha-bromonaphthalene, CCl_4 which are not to be used in medicinal products. But brominated oils can be used for the same purpose.

(b) Coalescence and Breaking

Creaming is different from breaking because creaming is a reversible process whereas breaking is irreversible. A uniform mixture is reconstituted from a creamed emulsion by agitation because the oil globules are still surrounded by a protective sheath of emulsifying agent. When breaking occurs, simple mixing fails to resuspend the globules in a stable emulsified form because the film surrounding the particles has been destroyed and the oil tends to coalesce.

The addition of chemical that is incompatible with emulsifying agent, destroy its emulsifying ability. Anionic and cationic surfactants cause such incompatibility. Proteins and non-ionic surface active agents are excellent media for bacterial growth. Temperature changes may denature protein emulsifiers and solubility of non-ionic emulgents change with a rise in temperature, heating above 70°C, destroys most emulsions. Freezing also cracks emulsion; this may be due to ice formed disrupting the interfacial film around the droplets.

An optimum degree of dispersion for each particular system exists for maximum stability. As in case of solid particles, if dispersion is non uniform, small particles wedge between large ones, permitting stronger cohesion so that internal phase coalesce easily. Thus moderately coarse uniform dispersion should have maximum stability. Viscosity alone does not produce stable emulsions; however viscous emulsion may be more stable than mobile ones by the virtue of the retardation of flocculation and coalescence. Probably an optimum rather than a high viscosity is needed to promote stability.

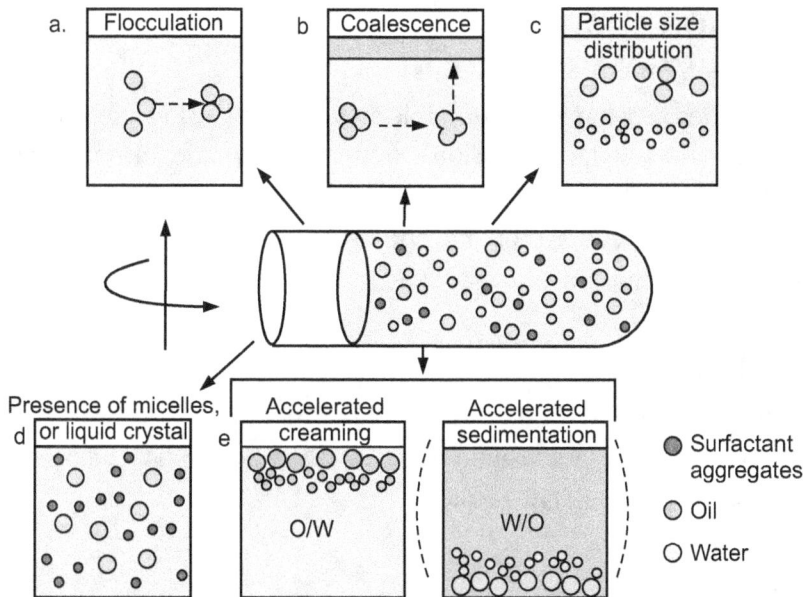

Fig. 3.6 : Physical Stability of Emulsions

(c) Phase Inversion

Although it was stated that stable emulsions containing more than 50 percent disperse phase are common, an attempt to incorporate excessive amounts of disperse phase may cause cracking of the emulsion or phase inversion (conversion of an o/w to w/o emulsion or vice versa). It can be shown that uniform spheres arranged in the closes packing will occupy 74.02 percent of total volume irrespective of their size.

Although it is possible to obtain more concentrated emulsions than this, because of the non uniformity of size of the globules and the possibility of deformation of shape of globules, there is tendency for emulsions containing more than about 70 percent disperse phase to crack or invert. This value is known as the critical point, is defined as the concentration of internal phase above which the emulsifying agent cannot produce a stable emulsion of desired type. Further, any additive that alters the HLB of an emulsifying agent may alter the emulsion type. The addition of magnesium salt to an emulsion stabilized with sodium oleate will cause the emulsion to crack. The addition of electrolyte to ionic and cationic surfactants may suppress their ionization owing to the common ion effect and so a w/o emulsion would be produced. Example: Turpentine liniment containing ammonium oleate and ammonium chloride (o/w → w/o). Emulsions stabilized with non-ionic emulsifying agents such as polysorbates may invert on heating. This is caused by breaking of hydrogen bond responsible for the hydrophilic characteristic of polysorbate, its HLB value is thus altered and emulsion inverts.

3.11 FORMULATION ADDITIVES

(I) Emulsifying agent/Emulsifiers/Emulgents

Emulsions are thermodynamically unstable systems so by using appropriate emulsifying agent to decrease the interfacial tension, the stability of the disperse system can be significantly increased. Stable emulsifier should have following properties:

- Have balance between hydrophilic and hydrophobic groups
- Produce stable emulsion
- Itself stable
- Chemically inert
- Nontoxic
- Cause no irritation on application
- Odourless, tasteless and colourless
- Inexpensive

Rule of Bancroft

Type of emulsion is a function of relative solubility of surfactant. The phase in which it is soluble becomes the continuous phase.

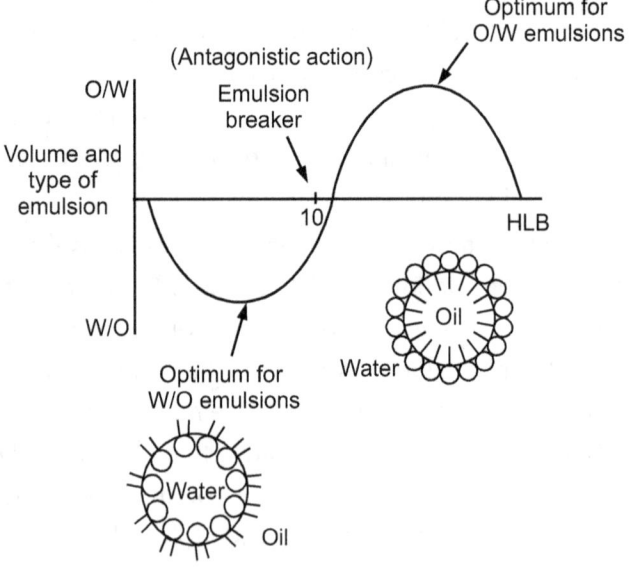

Fig. 3.7 : Types of Emulsion

Emulsifying agents are classified into following three groups.

1) **Surfactants:** Adsorbed at oil/water interfaces to form monomolecular film and reduces interfacial tension.

2) **Natural macromolecular material:** They form multimolecular films around the droplet of o/w emulsion and increase the viscosity of dispersion medium. But they have tendency to undergo hydrolysis and are sensitive to variation in pH.

3) **Very finely dispersed solid:** Adsorbed at the liquid/liquid interfaces, forming films of particles around the dispersed globules. The solid particle size must be very small as compared to droplet size and exhibit appropriate angle of contact at the three phases, oil/water/solid boundary. Example: Bentonite, Veegum, Colloidal silicon dioxide etc.

(1) Surfactants

(A) Synthetic/Semi-synthetic Surface Active Agent

Depending on their ionization in aqueous solution, these are classified as anionic, cationic, non-ionic and amphoteric surfactants.

(a) Anionic Surfactants

In aqueous solution these dissociate to form negatively charged ions/ions responsible for their emulsifying ability. Anionic surfactants are cheap but toxic hence, used only for external preparations only. Examples are,

(i) Alkali metal and ammonium soap: These are sodium, potassium or ammonium salts of long chain of fatty acids such as oleic acid, stearic acid etc. Example: sodium stearate gives o/w emulsion. When alkali reacts with fatty acid, internally lead to *in-situ* emulsification.

(ii) Soaps of divalent and trivalent metals: Although calcium, magnesium, aluminium and zinc salt of fatty acid are w/o emulsifying agents, only calcium salt is commonly used. Ca salt react with fatty acids, $Ca(OH)_2$ in combination with oleic acid gives o/w emulsion, Zinc cream B.P., Oily calamine lotion.

(iii) Amine soaps: They form o/w emulsion and applicable for external preparation only. They are compatible with acids and electrolytes. Example: Triethanol amines stearate.

(iv) Sulphated and sulphonated compounds: These are highly water soluble and have inability to form condensed film at o/w interface; hence they are used with non-ionic oil soluble emulsifying agents. Example: Sodium lauryl sulphate and Sodium cetostearyl sulphate.

(b) Cationic Surfactants

In aqueous solution these dissociate into a cation responsible for their emulsifier ability. Quaternary ammonium compounds are o/w emulsifying agents. They are used with non-ionic oil soluble auxiliary emulgent and give stable preparations. They are incompatible with anionic, polyvalent anions and at high pH. Example: Cetrimide.

(c) Nonionic Surfactants

Nonionic surfactants do not dissociate in aqueous solution. If these are oil soluble then it gives w/o emulsion and water soluble gives o/w emulsion. If we use combination of these two it will give complex film formation. These are less toxic, less irritant, hence used for oral, ophthalmic and parentral preparations and compatible with cationic, anionic, electrolyte and pH change. These are more expensive.

If surfactant is more hydrophobic it will go in oil phase and not concentrate at interface and vice versa. So equal balance of HLB, one hydrophilic and one hydrophobic surfactant and cohesion between their hydrocarbon chains will then hold both types of interface. Examples are :

1) **Glycol and glycerol esters (polyhydric alcohol and fatty acid ester):** As these are hydrophobic in nature they produce poor o/w emulsion when used alone. However when mixed with salts of fatty acids, the mixture is self emulsifying and can use as primary emulgent for o/w creams and lotions. Example: Glycerol monostearate, glycerol mono oleate, diethylene glycol monostearate, propylene glycol mono oleate etc.

2) **Sorbitan ester (Span):** Esterification of –OH group of sorbitan with lauric, oleic, palmitic or stearic acid give sorbitan ester and give w/o type of emulsion. Esterification of sorbitan with polysorbate give o/w or w/o type of emulsion. Example: Sorbitan trioleate (Span 85), Sorbitan mono oleate (Span 80), Sorbitan monostearate (Span 60), Sorbitan mono laurate (Span 20).

3) **Polysorbates (Tween):** Polysorbates are polyethylene glycol derivatives of sorbitan ester. The combination of polysorbate and sorbitan ester gives complex condensed film. Examples: Polyoxyethylene sorbitan monostearate (Polysorbate 60); Polyoxyethylene sorbitan mono oleate (Polysorbate 80 / Tween 80); Polyoxyethylene sorbitan mono laurate (Polysorbate 20 / Tween 20); Poly wax-mixture of cetyl alcohol and polyoxyethylene sorbitan ester is self emulsifying.

   Disadvantages:

   1. Unpleasant taste.
   2. Preservative is inactived by complexation with surfactant.

4) **Fatty alcohol and polyglycol ethers:** Macrogol, polymer of ethylene oxide contain many hydrophilic groups. Cetomacrogol (cetostearyl ether 22) is polyethylene glycol monocetyl ether. They are water soluble and hence produce o/w emulsion. These are stable over a wide range of pH.

5) **Poloxalkols/poloxamers :** Polyoxyethylene/polyoxypropylene copolymer.

(d) Amphoteric

They possess both positive and negative charge. At low pH, they are cationic in nature and vice versa. Example: Lecithine (IV fat emulsion stabilizer).

(B) Naturally Occurring Surfactants and their Derivatives

A variety of emulsifiers are natural products derived from plant or animal tissue. Most of the emulsifiers form hydrated lyophilic colloids (called hydrocolloids) that form multimolecular layers around emulsion droplets. Hydrocolloid type emulsifiers have little or no effect on interfacial tension, but exert a protective colloid effect, reducing the potential for coalescence, by:

- Providing a protective sheath around the droplets.
- Imparting a charge to the dispersed droplets (so that they repel each other).
- Swelling to increase the viscosity of the system (so that droplets are less likely to merge).

Disadvantages:

- Prone to microbial growth i.e. bacterial or moulds.
- Batch to batch composition variation.
1) **Polysaccharides:** Acacia is naturally occurring polysaccharide and forms multimolecular film and produce o/w type of emulsion but major disadvantage associated with acacia is that it is less viscous, hence always used in combination with tragacanth and sodium alginate.
2) **Semisynthetic polysaccharides:** They are free of batch to batch composition variation and give o/w type of emulsion. Example: Methyl cellulose, Cross CMC etc.
3) **Sterol containing substance:** Beeswax is used in cosmetics to produce o/w or w/o emulsion. Beeswax borax is incompatible for internal use due to toxicity. Wool fat (anhydrous Lanolin) has characteristic odour. Wool alcohol does not have characteristic odour.

(2) Hydrophilic Colloids (Natural Macromolecular Material)

These materials generally exhibit little surface activity, adsorb at the o/w interface and form multilayer. Such multilayer has viscoelastic properties, resist rupture and form mechanical barrier to coalescence. Example: proteins (gelatin, casein), polysaccharides (acacia, cellulose derivatives, alginates etc.) However, some of these substances have chemical group that ionize, thus providing electrostatic repulsion or barrier to coalescence. Example: acacia consists of salts of arabic acid, protein contains both amino acid and carboxylic acid group. Most cellulose derivatives are not charged and thus sterically stabilize the system.

Hydrocolloid emulsifiers may be classified as:

- Vegetable derivatives, Example: acacia, tragacanth, agar, pectin, carrageenan, lecithin.
- Animal derivatives, Example: gelatin, lanolin, cholesterol.
- Semi-synthetic agents, Example: methylcellulose, carboxymethylcellulose.
- Synthetic agents, Example: carbopols®

(3) Finely Divided or Finely Dispersed Solid Particle Emulsifiers

Emulsions may be stabilized by finely divided solid particles if they are preferentially wetted by one phase and possess sufficient adhesion for one another so that they form a film around the dispersed droplets. Solid particles will remain at the interface as long as a stable contact angle, θ is formed by liquid/liquid interface and solid surface. The liquid whose contact angle is less than 90° will form continuous phase. Aluminium and Magnesium hydroxide, clays such as bentonite, veegum, hectorite are wetted by water and therefore stabilize o/w emulsion. Example: liquid paraffin and magnesium hydroxide emulsion. Carbon black and talc are wetted by oils and stabilize w/o emulsion.

(4) Auxiliary Emulsifying Agents

A variety of fatty acids (Example: stearic acid), fatty alcohols (Example: stearyl or cetyl alcohol), and fatty esters (Example: glyceryl monostearate) serve to stabilize emulsions through their ability to thicken the emulsion. Because these agents have only weak emulsifying properties, they are always used in combination with other emulsifiers.

Combinations of emulsifiers can produce more stable emulsions than using a single emulsifier with the same HLB number. The HLB value of a combination of emulsifiers can be calculated as follows:

$$HLB = \frac{(\text{Quantity of surfactat 1})(\text{HLB surfactant 1}) + (\text{Quantity of surfactant 2}) (\text{HLB surfactant 2})}{\text{Quantity of surfactant 1} + \text{Quantity of surfactant 2}}$$

(II) Buffer

They are used to maintain the pH. They are chemically stable, physiologically compatible and have controlled toxicity. Example: phosphate, acetate buffer etc.

(III) Density Modifier

It is necessary to add density modifier to prevent creaming (arise due to density difference of both phases). Example: sucrose, dextrose, glycerol, propylene glycol etc.

(IV) Humectant

Humectants like glycerine, propylene glycol are added. About 5 percent in aqueous phase to prevent drying but high concentration of humectants used in topical preparation removes moisture from skin and causes dehydration.

(V) Antioxidants

Upon auto oxidation, unsaturated oils, such as vegetable oil, give rise to rancidity with resultant unpleasant odor, appearance and taste. It can be inhibited by the absence of oxygen, by a free radical chain breaker by reducing agent. Example: Butylated hydroxy anisole (BHA) (0.02 percent for fixed oils, fats and 0.1percent for essential oils), Butylated hydroxyl toluene (BHT), L tocopherol, esters of gallic acid (0.001 percent and 0.1 percent for essential oils). BHT and BHA have a pronounced odor and should be used at low concentration. Alkyl gallates have a bitter taste whereas L tocopherol is well suited for edible or oral preparation.

Almost all antioxidants are subjected to discoloration in the presence of light, trace metals and alkaline solution. Combination of two or more antioxidants has been shown to produce synergestic effects. In some cases, compounds completely devoid of antioxidant activity by themselves enhance the effectiveness of certain antioxidants. Example: alkali gallates, BHT, BHA are much more effective in the presence of citric acid, tartaric acid and phosphoric acid.

(VI) Preservatives

Microbial contamination may occur during the development of an emulsion or during its use. Requirements of preservatives are,

- Wide spectrum of activity i.e. effective against gram positive, negative bacteria, yeast, moulds.
- Bacteriostatic activity/no cidal activity.
- Non-toxic, non-irritant, non-sensitizing.
- Compatible with other emulgent. Example: phenols, methyl paraben are incompatible with non-ionic emulgents.
- High water soluble, low o/w partition coefficient
- Effective over a wide range of pH and temperature.

Complex problem arises whenever the preservative interact with one of the emulsion ingredients. To overcome this, usually excess of preservative is added after emulgent has concentrated at o/w interfaces. Example: Benzoic acid, ascorbic acid and its salts, parahydroxybenzoic acid, chlorocresol, quaternary ammonium compound etc. No single preservative have ideal characteristics hence, combination of preservatives is often used. Example: Methyl paraben to propyl paraben 10:1.

3.12 TECHNIQUES OF EMULSIFICATION

- Additions of the internal phase to the external phase, while subjecting the system to shear or fracture.
- Phase inversion technique - the external phase is added to the internal phase. Example: If an o/w emulsion is to be prepared, the aqueous phase is added to the oil phase.

- Mixing both phases after warming each. This method is frequently used in the preparation of ointments and creams (Beaker method).

- Alternate addition of the two phases to the emulsifying agent. In this method, the water and oil are added alternatively, in small portions, to the emulsifier. This technique is especially suitable for the preparation of food emulsions.

3.13 METHODS FOR EMULSION FORMULATION

1. Dry Gum Method (Continental Method)

The continental method is used to prepare the initial or primary emulsion from oil, water and a hydrocolloid or "gum" type emulsifier (usually acacia). The primary emulsion or emulsion nucleus is formed from 4 parts of oil, 2 parts of water and one part of gum. The 4 parts of oil and 1 part of gum represent their total amount for the final emulsion.

In a mortar, one part of gum (acacia) is to be levitated with four parts of oil until the powder is thoroughly wetted; then the two parts water should be added all at once and the mixture is vigorously and continuously triturated until the primary emulsion is form, creamy white in appearance and produces a "crackling" sound as it is triturated (usually 3-4 minutes).

Additional water or aqueous solutions may be incorporated after the primary emulsion is formed. Solid substances (Example: active ingredients, preservatives, color, flavors etc.) are generally added as a solution to the primary emulsion; oil soluble substances in small amounts may be incorporated directly into the primary emulsion. Any substance which might reduce the physical stability of the emulsion, such as alcohol (which may precipitate the gum) should be added as near to the end of the process as possible to avoid breaking of the emulsion. When all agents have been incorporated, the emulsion should be transferred to a calibrated vessel, brought to final volume with water, then homogenized or blended to ensure uniform distribution of ingredients. Ratio of oil: gum: water in primary emulsion for various types of oils is as follows,

Fixed oil = 4:1:2, Mineral oil = 3:1:2, Volatile oil = 2:1:2 and Oleo gum resin = 1:1:2

2. Wet Gum Method (English Method)

The proportion of oil and water and emulsifier (gum) are the same as in dry gum method, but the order and technique of mixing are different. The gum is triturated with water to form mucilage; then oil is to be added slowly in portions, while triturating. After all the oil is added, the mixture should be triturated for several minutes to form the primary emulsion. Then other ingredients are added as in continental method. This method is more difficult to perform successfully, especially with more viscous oils, but may result in a more stable emulsion.

3. Bottle Method

This method is used to prepare emulsions of volatile oils, or oliogeneous substances of vary low viscosities. In this, gum is to be placed in a dry bottle and oil is added. Then the bottle is capped and should be shaken thoroughly. Into this the required volume of water is to be added all at once and the mixture is shaken thoroughly until the primary emulsion is formed. It is important to minimize the initial amount of time for the mixing of gum and oil. The gum will tend to imbibe the oil and will become water proof.

4. Beaker Method

When synthetic or non-gum emulsifiers are used, the proportions given in the previous methods become meaningless. The most appropriate method for preparing emulsions from surfactants or other non-gum emulsifiers is to begin by dividing components into water soluble and oil soluble components. All oil soluble components are dissolved in the oily phase in one beaker and all water soluble components are dissolved in the water in a separate beaker. Oleaginous components are melted and both phases are heated to approximately at 70°C over a water bath. The internal phase is then added to the external phase with stirring until the product reaches room temperature. The mixing of such emulsions can be carried out in a beaker, mortar, or blender; or, in the case of creams and ointments, in the jar in which they will be dispensed.

3.14 EQUIPMENTS FOR EMULSION MANUFACTURING

3.14.1 Agitators

Agitation or shaking may be used to prepare the emulsion. This method is frequently employed by the pharmacist, particularly in the emulsification of easily dispersed, low viscosity oils. Under certain conditions, intermittent shaking is considerably more effective than ordinary continuous shaking. Continuous shaking tends to break up not only the phase to be dispersed but also the dispersion medium, thus impairing the ease of emulsification; laboratory shaking devices may be used for small scale production.

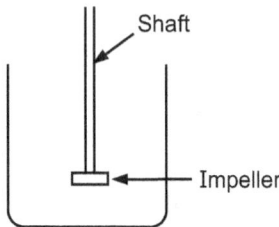

Fig. 3.8 : Agitator

3.14.2 Mechanical Mixers

Emulsion may be prepared by using one of several mixers that are available. Propeller type mixers that have a propeller attached to a shaft driven by an electric motor are convenient and portable and can be used for both stirring and emulsification. This type operates best in mixtures that have low viscosity, that is, mixture with a viscosity of glycerine or less. They are also useful for preparing emulsions. Turbine mixers have a number of blades that may be straight or curved, with or without pitch, mounted on a shaft. The turbine tends to give a greater shear than propellers. The shear can be increased by using diffuser rings that are perforated and surround the turbine so that the liquid from the turbine must pass through holes. The turbine can be used for both low viscosity mixtures and medium viscosity liquids, up to that of molasses. The degree of stirring and shear by propeller turbine mixers depends upon several factors, such as the speed of rotation, pattern of liquid flow, position in the container.

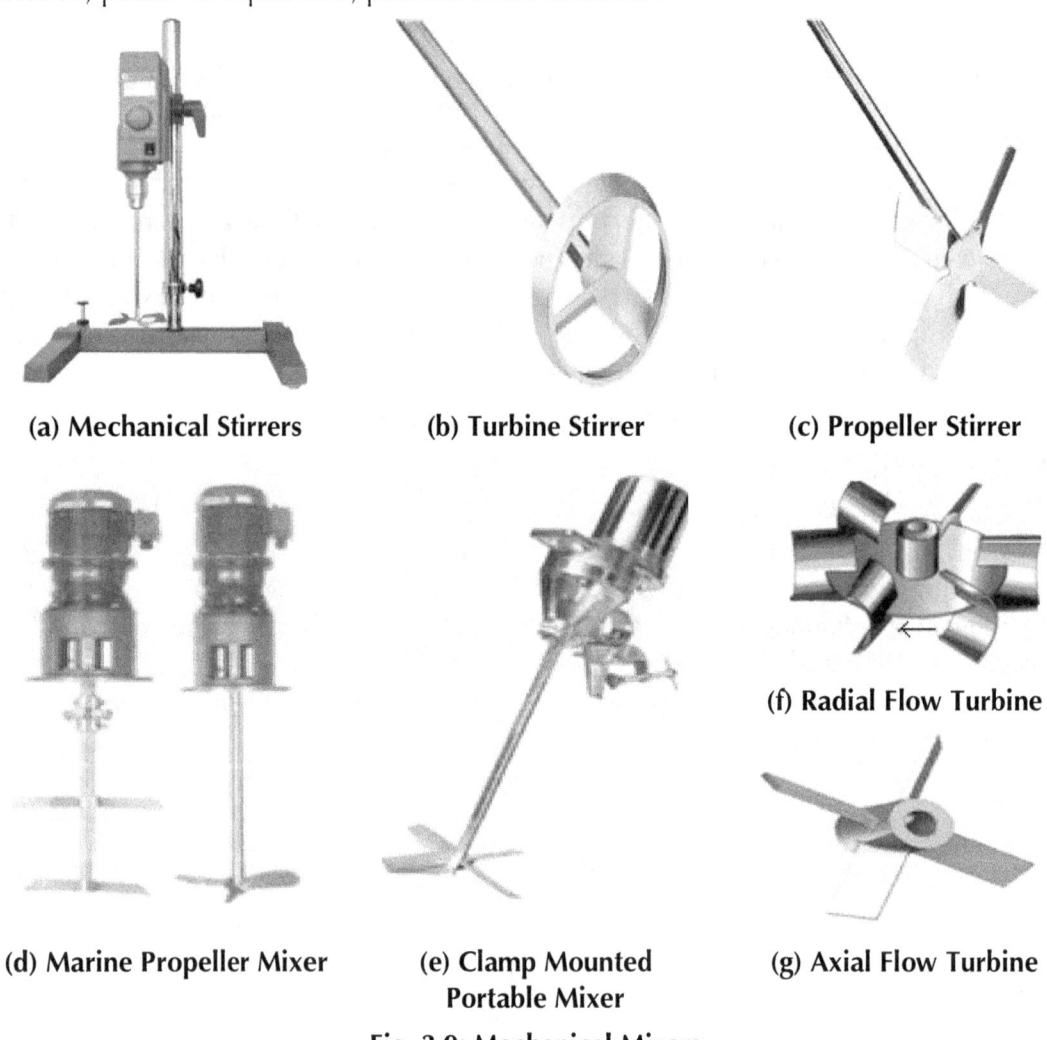

(a) Mechanical Stirrers   **(b) Turbine Stirrer**   **(c) Propeller Stirrer**

(f) Radial Flow Turbine

(d) Marine Propeller Mixer   **(e) Clamp Mounted Portable Mixer**   **(g) Axial Flow Turbine**

Fig. 3.9: Mechanical Mixers

3.14.3 Colloid Mills

In this, mixed phases of an emulsion formula are passed between a stator and a high speed rotor revolving at speeds of 2000 to 18,000 rpm. The clearance between the rotor and stator is adjustable, usually from 0.001 in upward. The emulsion mixture, passing between rotor and stator, is subjected to a tremendous shearing action that effects a fine dispersion of uniform size. The shearing force applied in the colloid mill usually result in temperature rise within the emulsion. It may be necessary, therefore, to cool the equipment when the emulsion is being produced. Droplet size of emulsion can be determined by shear force within the gap between the spinning rotor and stationary rotor. Droplets size decreases with homogenization intensity and with decreasing viscosity of the dispersed phase.

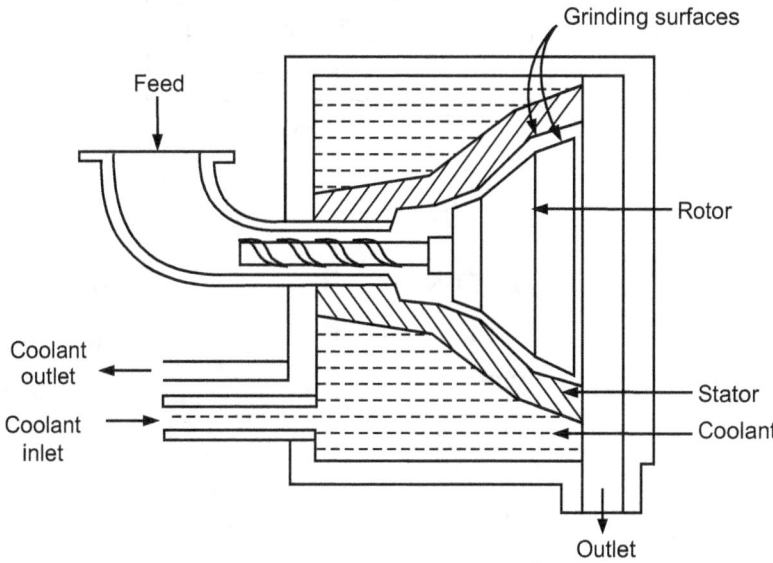

Fig. 3.10: Colloid Mill

3.14.4 Homogenizers

Homogenizers may be used in one of the two ways:

- The ingredients in the emulsions are mixed and then passed through the homogenizer to produce the final product

- A coarse emulsion is prepared in some other way and then passed through a homogenizer for the purpose of decreasing the particle size and obtaining a greater degree of uniformity and stability.

The mixed phases or the coarsed emulsions are subjected to homogenization and are passed between a finely ground valve and seat under high pressure. This, in effect, produces an atomization that is enhanced by the impact received by the atomized mixture as it strikes the surrounding metal surface that operate at pressure of 1000-5000 per square inch and produce some of the finest dispersions obtainable in an emulsion. It is postulated that circulation and turbulence are responsible mainly for the homogenization. Two-stage homogenizers are constructed so that the emulsion, after treatment in the first valve system, is conducted directly to another where it receives a second treatment.

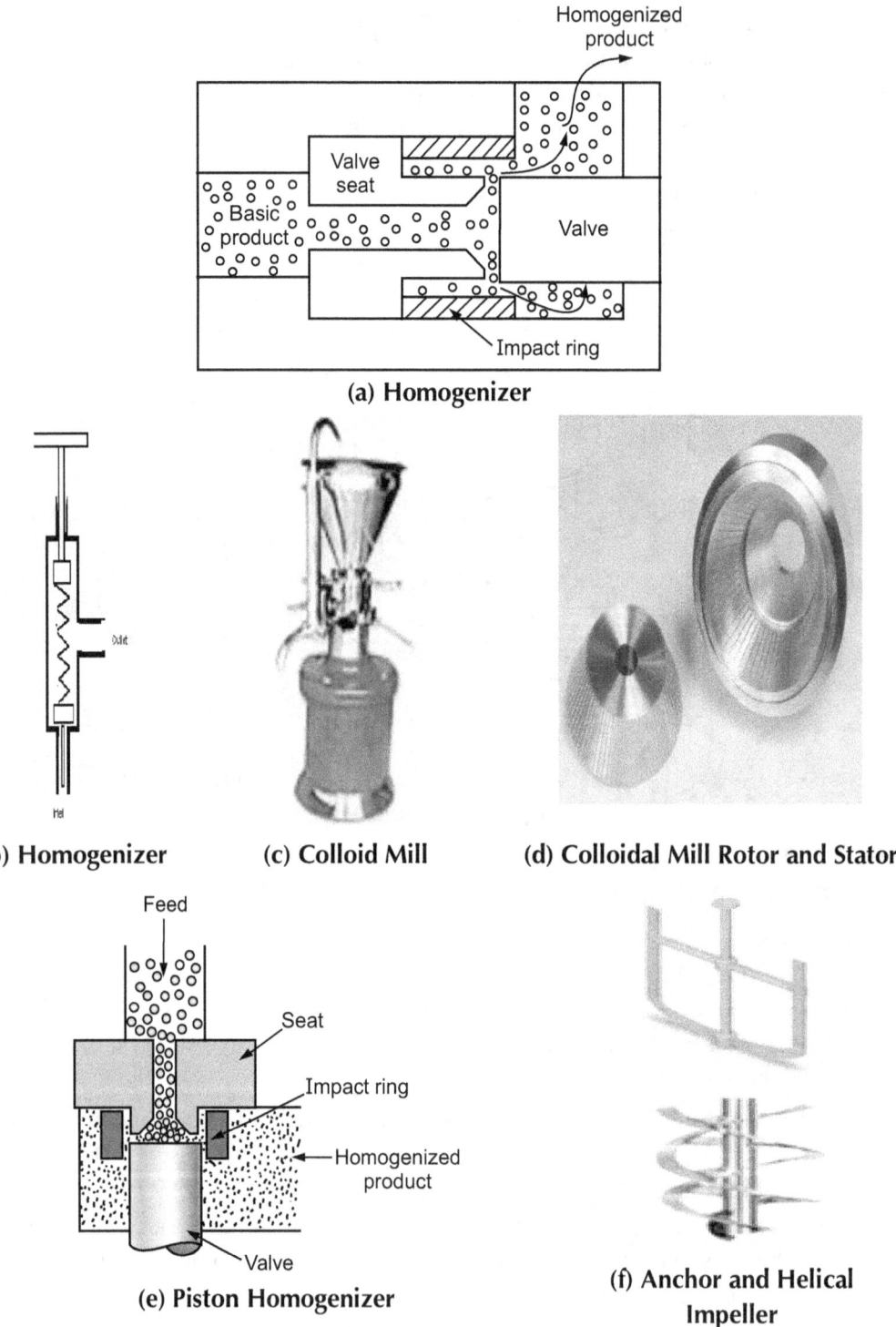

(a) Homogenizer

(b) Homogenizer   (c) Colloid Mill   (d) Colloidal Mill Rotor and Stator

(e) Piston Homogenizer

(f) Anchor and Helical Impeller

Fig. 3.11: Homogenizers

3.14.5 Ultrasonic Devices

Commercial products may be prepared by using ultrasonic based upon the device known as the Pohlman whistle. In this apparatus, the premixed liquids are forced through a thin orifice and are allowed to impinge upon the free end of a knife-edge bar that is made to vibrate. Ultrasonic waves are produced and areas of compression and rarefaction are formed. Shock waves are produced by the collapse of bubbles that produce a shear effect, thereby producing fine particle sizes.

3.15 MULTIPLE EMULSION

Multiple emulsions are more complex systems. When a simple emulsion is further dispersed within another continuous phase, the system formed is called multiple emulsion.

Schematically the preparation of w/o/w emulsion is as follows:

Aqueous Phase

↓

Oil + Lipophilic surfactant

↓ Mix, Homogenization

w/o emulsion

↓

Aqueous solution containing hydrophilic surfactant

↓ Mix

w/o/w multiple emulsion

Step 1: Aqueous phase is added to an oily phase, containing lipophilic surfactant. Forms w/o emulsion upon mixing.

Step 2: The above formed (w/o) emulsion is added to second aqueous solution containing hydrophilic surfactant which upon mixing gives the multiple w/o/w emulsion. The two basic types of multiple emulsions are (i) w/o/w - water in oil in water (ii) o/w/o - oil in water in oil.

Recently multiple emulsions have been developed with the purpose of prolonging the release of drugs incorporated. This has gain interest for microencapsulation of peptides/proteins and hydrophilic drugs. They have used to increase the encapsulation efficiency of hydrophilic compounds. w/o/w, o/w/o, w/o/o, w/o/o/o emulsions have been used.

Mixed emulsions can also invert; however during inversion they usually form simple emulsions. Thus w/o/w emulsions normally yield an o/w emulsions. The particle size of dispersed phase determines the appearance of the emulsion. Droplet ranges from 0.25 to 10u. The double emulsion has found special use as extraction systems.

Stability of Three Phase Emulsion

Generally, a two phase emulsion will separate into two clear layers, with one interface between them. The emulsion discussed in this separate into three phases, which means two interfaces are found at separation. Several examples of three phase emulsion are provided but three main categories have been chosen in which the third phase is respectively a solid, a liquid or a liquid crystal. The three cases impart different properties to the emulsion.

(A) When Third Phase – a Solid

Solid particles are often a part of emulsion formation and the simultaneous stabilization of it causes problems. In fact, the solid particles may be used to stabilize an emulsion due to their ability to be wetted by the two phases. They will stabilize the emulsion if they are located at the interface between the two liquids. At the interface they serve as a mechanical barrier to prevent the coalescence of droplets.

If electrically charged, against a continuous aqueous phase, the electrical double layer will further assist in the stabilization against flocculation. (This is generally in 2 phase systems).

The protection against coalescence is based on the energy to expel the particles from the interface into dispersed droplets and this energy is dependent upon contact angle and can be calculated as,

$$\Delta e = \pi r^2_\rho r_{o/w} \ (1 - \cos \theta)^2$$

where Δe = energy to expel spherical droplet

   r = radius from the interface into the phase by which it is predominantly wet and towards its contact angle

   $r_{o/w}$ = the interfacial tension between oil and water phase

Practically the value of θ should be maximum 90° while theoretically it increases to 180° which is not correct. An oil-water-solid contact angle of θ = 90° means that the particles as such are optimally stabilized.

If the contact angle toward water is less than 90°, an oil soluble surfactant is added and if θ exceeds, a water soluble surfactant is added to reduce the interfacial free energy between water and the solid by reducing θ. Thus, the stabilization is achieved if the third phase is a solid.

(B) When Third Phase - a Liquid

The third phase is very useful case because it allows low energy emulsification. The basic background follows:

At low temperature, below the cloud point (the temperature above which nonionic surfactant of this kind ceases to be water soluble at low concentration) these surfactants are preferentially water soluble, hence they are heavily partitioned towards the aqueous phase.

At high temperature, above the cloud point the surfactant solubility in water is extremely small and it is then partitioned almost entirely into oil. At intermediate temperature, the HLB temperature or the phase inversion temperature (PIT), a third phase, the surfactant phase, appears between the oil and the water.

Water, hydrocarbon and a nonionic surfactant form two phase at low and high temperature. In a small temperature range, three liquid phases are found in the HLB temperature range.

The key to low energy emulsification is to emulsify at this HLB temperature and to follow this by rapid cooling to about 25-30°C. For an o/w emulsion to be used at room temperature, the HLB temperature should be approximately 55°C. A w/o emulsion requires opposite conditions.

(C) When Third Phase - a Liquid Crystal

In addition to micelles and microemulsion droplets, surfactant may form liquid crystal, of which one with a layered structure is most important for emulsion science. In a liquid crystal, the chains are in liquid state and the diffusion along the layers is of the same magnitude as in a liquid.

The introduction of liquid crystals as a stabilizing element for emulsions occur in 1969, when it was found that the sudden stabilization at emulsifier concentration in excess 2.5 per cent of a water–p-xylene emulsion by a commercial octaethylene glycol nonphenyl ether, was due to the formation of a liquid crystalline phase in the emulsion.

The essential features of such emulsion are:

1] The structure of the liquid crystal.
2] Its stabilizing action.
3] The specific applications of such emulsion.
4] Useful surfactant.

3.16 MICROEMULSION

Microemulsions are isotropic, thermodynamically stable transparent (or translucent) systems of oil, water and surfactant, frequently in combination with a co-surfactant with a droplet size usually in the range of 20-200 nm. These homogeneous systems, which can be prepared over a wide range of surfactant concentration and oil to water ratio, are all fluids of low viscosity. Microemulsions are easy to administer to children and to people who have difficulty in swallowing solid oral dosage forms. Microemulsions are dynamic systems in which the interface is continuously and spontaneously fluctuating. Structurally, they are divided into oil-in-water (o/w), water-in-oil (w/o) and bi-continuous microemulsions. In w/o microemulsions, water droplets are dispersed in the continuous oil phase while o/w microemulsion is formed when oil droplets are dispersed in the continuous aqueous phase.

In systems where the amounts of water and oil are similar, a bi-continuous microemulsion may result. In all three types of microemulsions, the interface is stabilized by an appropriate combination of surfactants and/or co-surfactants.

Microemulsions as drug delivery tool show favourable properties like thermodynamic stability (long shelf-life), easy formation (zero interfacial tension and almost spontaneous formation), optical isotropy, ability to be sterilized by filtration, high surface area (high solubilization capacity) and very small droplet size.

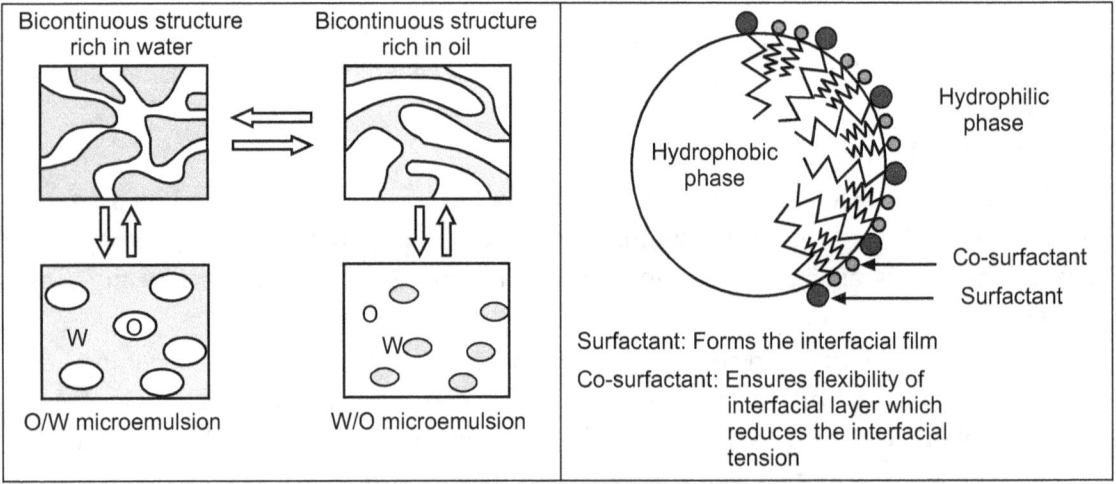

Fig. 3.12: Microemulsion Microstructures

Table 3.3 : Properties of Micoemulsion and Emulsion

Sr. No.	Property	Microemulsion	Emulsion
1.	Physical appearance	Transparent (or transluscent)	Cloudy
2.	Optical isotropy	Isotropic	Anisotropic
3.	Interfacial tension	Ultra low	High
4.	Microstructure	Dynamic	Static
5.	Droplet size	20-200 nm	> 500 nm

Contd...

6.	Stability	Thermodynamically stable, long shelf-life	Thermodynamically unstable (kinetically stable)
7.	Phases	Monophasic	Biphasic
8.	Preparation cost	Facile preparation, relatively lower cost for commercial production.	Require a large input of energy, higher cost.
9.	Viscosity	Low viscosity with Newtonian behaviour	Higher viscosity

Formulation of Microemulsions

The main components of microemulsion system are: 1) Oil phase, 2) Primary surfactant, 3) Secondary surfactant (co-surfactant), 4) Co-solvent.

Table 3.4 : Commonly used Components for Microemulsions

Components		Examples
Oils	LCDs	Corn oil, soyabean oil, safflower oil, olive oil, etc.
	MCTs	Glyceryl tricaprylate/caprate : Captex 355, Miglyol 810, Neobee M-5, etc.
	Mono/di glycerides	Glyceryl caprylate/caprate (Capmul MCM), Glycerol monooleate (Capmul GMO), etc.
	Fatty acids	Oleic acid
Surfactants	Propylene glycol esters	Capmul PG-8, Propylene glycol monolauate (Lauroglycol)
	HLB < 10	Phosphatidylcholine (Phospholipon), Unsaturated polyglycolized glycerides (Labrafil M2125). Sorbitan monopalmitate (Span 40), Sorbitan monooleate (Span 80), etc.
	HLB > 10	Polyoxyethylene 20 sorbitan monolaurate (Tween 20), Polyoxyethylene 20 sorbitan monooleate (Tween 80), Polyoxyl 35 castor oil (Cremophore EL), PEG-8 caprylic/capric glycerides (Labrasol), Polyoxyl 40 hydrogenated castor oil (Cremophore RH 40), etc.
Co-solvents	Propylene glycol, Polyethylene glycol, Ethanol, etc.	

Characterization of Microemulsions

- Phase Behavior Studies
- Droplet Size and Shape
- Nuclear Magnetic Resonance Studies
- Interfacial Tension
- Viscosity
- Dye Solubilization
- Electron Microscope Characterization
- Stability Studies

3.17 ASSESSMENT OF EMULSION – SHELF LIFE

(I) Stress Conditions

Stress conditions are normally employed for evaluating stability of emulsion.

(a) Aging and Temperature

Generally, shelf life of all type of preparation can be determined by storing them for varying periods of time at temperature higher than normal. In case of emulsion, change in temperature leads to new reaction. It is clearly established that many emulsions may be perfectly stable at 40° / 45° C, but cannot tolerate temperature in excess of 55° or 60° even for few hours. Varied effect of temperature changes on emulsion parameter have been discussed before such as viscosity, partitioning of emulsifiers, inversion at phase inversion temperature and crystallization of certain lipids.

Particularly, a useful means of evaluating shelf life is cycling between two temperatures. Again, extremes should be avoided and cycling should be conducted between 4° and 45° C. The normal effect of aging on emulsion at elevated temperature is acceleration of rate of coalescence or creaming, this is usually coupled with change in viscosity. Most emulsions become thinner at elevated temperature and thicken when allowed to come to room temperature. Freezing can damage more than heating, since solubility of emulsifiers in lipid and aqueous phase is more sensitive to freezing than modest warming.

(b) Centrifugation/Gravitation

Shelf life under normal storage conditions can be predicted rapidly, by observing separation of dispersed phase due to either creaming or coalescence, when emulsion is exposed to centrifugation. Stokes's law shows that creaming is a function of gravity. Therefore increase in gravity accelerates separation. Centrifugation at 3750 rpm in 10 cm radius centrifuge for period of five hours is equivalent to effect of gravity for about one year. Ultracentrifugation of emulsion creates 3 layers :(a) top layer of coagulated oil, (b) intermediate layer of uncoagulated emulsion and (c) pure aqueous layer.

The rate of oil formation in nujol: water: sodium dodecyl sulphate (50:50:0.2percent) emulsion depends on rate of centrifugation. Separation was extremely rapid at 56,000 rpm. Somewhat slower at about 40,000 rpm and no oil was separated after two and half hour of centrifugation at approximately 11,000 rpm. These findings suggest that force of ultracentrifugation does not cause oil separation until it is high enough to break or rupture the absorbed layer of emulsifier that surrounds each droplet. It is concluded that centrifugation is an extremely useful tool for evaluating and predicting shelf life of emulsions.

(c) Agitation

The droplet in an emulsion exhibits Brownian movement. In fact, it is believed that no coalescence of droplet takes place unless droplets impinge upon each owing to their Brownian movement. Excessive shaking of emulsion or excessive homogenization may interfere with formation of emulsion. As a result, agitation can also break emulsions.

(II) Chemical Parameters

It is necessary to ensure that any emulgent system used is physically and chemically compatible with an active agent and other emulsion ingredients. Example: ionic emulsifying agent is incompatible with materials of opposite charge and anionic and cationic emulgent are thus mutually incompatible. Already, it has been demonstrated that presence of electrolyte can influence stability of emulsion by either, (a) reducing energy of interaction between adjacent globules and (b) a salting out effect, by which high concentration of electrolyte can strip emulsifying agent on their hydrated layers and so cause their precipitation. In some cases phase inversion may occurs rather than demulsification. Example: sodium soap is used to stabilize o/w emulsion. Then addition of divalent electrolyte such as calcium chloride may form calcium soap which stabilize w/o emulsion.

Emulgents may also be precipitated by addition of materials in which they are insoluble. It may be possible to precipitate hydrophilic alcohol by addition of alcohol. Change in pH may lead to breaking of emulsion. Soap stabilized emulsions are therefore usually formulated at alkaline pH.

Oxidation

Many of the oil fat used in emulsion formulation are from animal or vegetable origin. They are susceptible to oxidation by atmospheric oxygen or by action of micro-organisms. The resulting rancidity leads to formation of degradation product of unpleasant odour and taste. Oxidation of microbial origin is controlled by use of antimicrobial preservatives and atmospheric oxidation by using reducing agents or using antioxidants.

(III) Physical Parameters

Most useful parameters commonly measured to assess the effect of stress conditions on emulsion include:

a) Phase separation

b) Viscosity

c) Electrophoretic properties

d) Particle size analysis and particle count

(a) Phase Separation

The rate and extent of phase separation after aging of an emulsion may be observed visually or by measuring the volume of separated phase. A study of mineral oil–water emulsion stabilized with either polyoxyethylene sorbitan monooleate or sodium laurel sulphate showed that the amount of coalescence observed at room temperature depends on concentration of emulsifier. At low level (below 0.1percent), visible coalescence of oil phase occurs after only one month's storage. At concentration of 2/5 percent, amount of visible coalescence is negligible even after two years storage.

A particularly simple means of determining phase separation involves withdrawing small specimens of emulsion from top and bottom of preparation after some period of storage and comparing composition of two samples by appropriate analysis of water content, oil content or any suitable constituent.

(b) Viscosity

Shelf life studies of emulsion are concerned with changes in viscosity during aging. Emulsion is generally non-Newtonian. Cone plate type viscometers are used to determine change of viscosity with age. In freshly prepared w/o emulsion, flocculation causes quick decrease in viscosity following a constant value. O/W emulsion shows increase in viscosity with flocculation. Consistency changes with time.

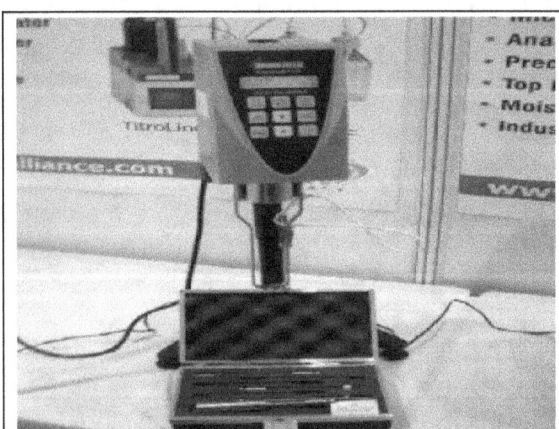

Fig. 3.13 (a): Brookfield Viscometer

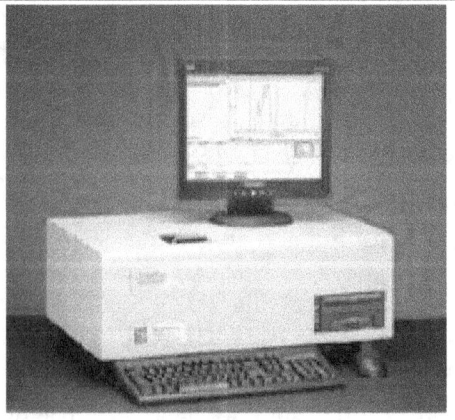

(b) Zeta Plus

Changes in viscosity with age help to determine the creaming or sedimentation at their early stages. Brookfield viscometer can be used. The descending rotating spindle of viscometer meets varying resistances at different levels and records fluctuations in viscosity. As high viscosity near the top is due to creaming while high viscosity at bottom is due to sedimentation. Viscosity changes can be related to particle size changes. Decrease in viscosity with age reflects an increase in particle size due to coalescence and then instability.

(c) Electrophoretic Properties

The zeta potential of emulsions can be measured with the aid of moving boundary method or more quickly and directly by observing the movement of particles under influence of electric current. Zeta potential is especially useful for assessing flocculation since electrical charges on particles influence the rate of flocculation. The measurement of electrical conductivity has been claimed to be a powerful tool for the evaluation of emulsion stability shortly after the preparation. Measurements are made on emulsions stored for short period of time at room temperature or 37°C. Conductivity depends on degree of dispersion. O/W preparation with fine particles exhibits low resistance. If resistance increases, it is sign of oil droplet aggregation and instability. A fine emulsion of water in w/o product does not conduct current until droplet coagulation i.e. instability occurs.

(d) Particle Size Number Analysis

Changes of average particle size or of size distribution of droplet are important for evaluating emulsions. Particle size analysis can be carried out by different methods like,

a) Microscopic measurement

b) Electronic counting device

c) Light scattering and related reflectance relationship

Change of reflectance at wavelength at which coloured internal phase partially absorbs incident light has been found to be inversely proportional to power of particle diameter. Utility of particle size for predicting or interpreting emulsion half life is doubtful. Two studies have shown that initial increase in particle size is rather rapid, but is followed by much slow change.

(IV) Microbial Contamination

The contamination of emulsion by micro-organism can adversely affect physicochemical properties of products, causing such a problem as gas production, colour and odour change, hydrolysis of fat and oil, pH changes in aqueous phase and breaking of emulsion. Some of the hydrophilic colloids, which are widely used as emulsifying agent, may provide a suitable nutritive medium for use by bacteria and moulds. Species of genus

Pseudomonas can utilize polysorbate aliphatic hydrocarbons and compounds. Some fixed oil, including arachis oil, can be used by some *Aspergillus* and *Rhizopus* species and liquid paraffin by some species of *Penicillium*. Oil in water emulsion tend to be more susceptible to microbial spoilage than water in oil products as, in latter case the continuous oil phase act as a barrier to spread of micro-organism throughout the product. Therefore it is necessary to include antimicrobial agent to prevent growth of any micro-organism in oil in water emulsion.

Adverse Storage Conditions

Adverse storage conditions may also cause emulsion instability. Increase in temperature will cause in increase in rate of creaming, leads to fall in apparent viscosity of continuous phase. Temperature increase will also cause increased kinetic motion, both of dispersed droplets and emulsifying agent at o/w interface. Certain macromolecular emulsifying agent may also be coagulated by increase in temperature while some emulgent may precipitate at low temperature.

Practical Recommendations for Shelf Life Predictions

Instability under stress can be related to normal shelf life. Therefore, it is important to set up a realistic stability program to assess the shelf life of emulsions. The emulsion should be stable with no visible signs of separation for at least 60-90 days at 45 or 50°C, 5-6 months at 37°C, and 12-18 months at room temperature. Similarly, there should be no visible signs of separation after 1 month storage 4°C and preferable after 2-3 freeze thaw cycles between –20 and +25°C. An emulsion should survive at least 6 or 8 hours heating or cooling cycles between refrigerator temperatures and 45°C with storage at each temperature of no less than 48 hours. A stable emulsion should not show any serious deterioration by centrifuging at 2000-3000 rpm at room temperature. The emulsion should not be adversely affected by agitation for 24-48 hours on a reciprocating shaker (approximately 60 cycles per minute at room temperature and 45°C). During testing period just described, sample stored at various conditions should be observed critically for separation and in addition, monitored at reasonable time interval for following characteristics:

   (a) Change in electrical conductivity

   (b) Change in light reflection

   (c) Change in viscosity

   (d) Change in particle size

   (e) Change in chemical composition

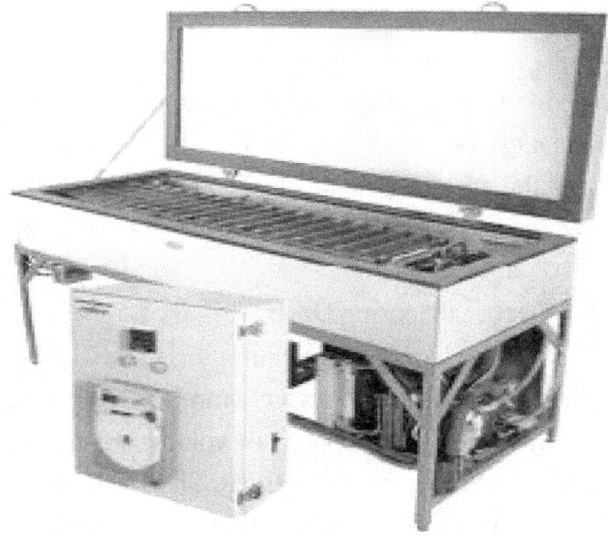

Fig. 3.14 : Freeze-Thaw Testing Freezer

3.18 CHARACTERIZATION OF DISPERSED SYSTEM (SUSPENSION AND EMULSION)

I) Particle Size Analysis

Particle size measurements provide the evaluation of possible particle aggregation or crystal growth. Particle size distribution data is employed as quality control standards. A wide particle size distribution promotes uneven settling in suspensions and coalescence in emulsions.

(i) Microscopy

Microscope helps in evaluation of particle diameter. One advantage of the optical method is to obtain information about the particle shape and presence of particle aggregations. A disadvantage is that the diameter is obtained from only two (of the three) dimensions of the particle i.e., length and breadth, not from thickness and width. Scanning electron microscopy (SEM) and transmission electron microscopy (TEM) are commonly used technologies.

(ii) Sieve Analysis

It is based on either vibratory or suction principles. In vibratory sieve analysis, selected number and size of sieves are stacked upon one another, with largest at the top. The known amount of sample is to place and vibrated in a mechanical device for determined time. The results can be obtained by weighing the amount retained on each sieve. The suction method uses one sieve at a time and examines the amount retained on the screen. The data is expressed as frequency or cumulative frequency plots, respectively.

(iii) Sedimentation Method

In sedimentation method, Anderson pipette and the Cahn sedimentation balance are used. The Anderson pipette involves measuring the percentage of solid that settle with time in a graduated sedimentation vessel. Solid samples are withdrawn from bottom of the vessel using a pipette and the amount of solids is determined by drying and weighing. The Cahn sedimentation balance electronically records the amount of dispersed powder settling out as a function of time.

(iv) Coulter Counter and Electrical Sensing Devices

Counters such as the Coulter counter determine the number of particles in a known volume of an electrolyte solution. The device employs the electrolyte displacement method and measures the equivalent spherical volume diameter, dv. This type of equipment is used primarily to obtain the particle size distribution of the sample. It measures the change in an electrical sensing zone when a particle passes through orifice positioned between two electrodes. The instrument is capable of counting particles at the rate of approximately 4000/sec and so both gross counts and particle size distributions are obtained in a relatively short period of time. Electronic pulse counters are also useful in studying particle growth, dissolution and particulate contamination.

(v) Light Scattering

The quasi-elastic light scattering technique (QELS)/photon correlation spectroscopy (PSC), is based on the principle of light scattering and has been employed to determine the mean particle diameter and size distribution (polydispersity). QELS has been used in the examination of heparin aggregates in commercial preparation. The method is applicable for measuring the particle size ranging from five nm to approximately three um. In this size range, the particles exhibit Brownian motion as a result of collision with the molecules of surrounding liquid medium, which cause fluctuation in the intensity of scattered light.

II) Determination of Electrical Properties/Zeta Potential

The movement of charged particles with respect to an adjacent liquid phase is the basic principle underlying four electrokinetic phenomena that are as follows:

- Electrophoresis
- Electro osmosis
- Sedimentation potential and
- Streaming potential

Electrophoresis involves the movement of a charged particle through a liquid under the influence of an applied potential difference. In the case of Electro osmosis, the particles are rendered immobile by forming a capillary or porous plug. The liquid moves through the plug or membrane, across which a potential is applied. The rate of flow of liquid through the plug can be determined under standard operating conditions.

Streaming potential is created by forcing a liquid to flow through a plug or bed of particles. Whereas, for the measurement of colloidal particles in the systems with low solids content, zeta potential can be determined by measuring the electrophoretic mobility of disperse particles in a charged electric field. Sedimentation potential measures the potential generated when the particles undergo sedimentation.

The determination of zeta potential of particles in a disperse system gives idea about the sign and magnitude of the charge and its effect on the stability of the system. It can be of value in the development of pharmaceutical suspension, particularly if the controlled aggregation approach is used. A number of semi-automated or fully automated instruments are recently used for studying the electrokinetic properties in the systems with high solids content. These include electrophoretic mass transport analyzer (zeta potential analyzer), the streaming current detector, the electrokinetic sonic amplitude device. While Zeta Reader, Zeta Meter, Laser Zee Meter are more useful for the measurement of colloidal particles in systems with low solid contents.

III) Rheological Measurements

The adequacy of hydration and quality control of the gums used as viscosity imparting agents in the products is best confirmed by a rheological test. In addition, the degree of dispersion, particle size and size distribution influence the viscosity and dispersion consistency. Increasing amounts of solid particles leads to increased viscosities of the dispersed system. The viscosity of lyophobic dispersions is not much higher than that of original liquid because of minimal interaction between the internal and external phase. The viscosity of lyophilic systems, especially polymer solution, is much higher because of the interaction between the two phases.

The instrument should provide the required rheological data over the desired range of shear, time under shear rate, time and temperature. Viscometers are classified as those that operate at a single shear rate and those that allow more than one rate of shear to be examined. Example bubble, cup, falling ball, falling rod and capillary viscometers.

Most rheometers in use to date are based on rotating the samples and measuring its response to the applied stress by a variety of sensor. The advantage of rotational viscometers are that the shear rate can be varied over a wide range and that continuous measurement at a given shear rate or shear stress can be made for extended periods of time, allowing the evaluation of time-dependency and shear-dependency properties. Simple rotational viscometers are the stormer viscometer, the ICI viscometer and the

Brookfield viscometer. Cone and plate and parallel plate rheometers are designed to handle small quantity samples, from about 0.2 to 5 ml.

IV) Temperature and Gravitational Stress Tests

Disperse systems can be subjected to cyclic temperature testing i.e. to conditions of repeated freezing and thawing (–50°C to + 40°C in 24 hours) exposing them to elevated temperatures (> 40°C) for short periods of storage to test for the physical stability. The use of stressful aging tests, however, has one advantage. If a given suspension is able to withstand exposure to extreme temperature, it is safe to assume that the product will have good physical stability during prolonged storage at ambient temperature.

CHAPTER 4

SEMISOLID DOSAGE FORMS

Contents

4.1   Introduction

4.2   Anatomy and Physiology of the Skin

    4.2.1 Layers of the Skin

    4.2.2 Functions of the Skin

4.3   Ideal Properties of Semisolid Dosage Forms

    4.3.1 Ideal Molecular Properties for Drug Penetration

4.4   Types of Conventional Semisolid Dosage Forms

4.5   Percutaneous Absorption

    4.5.1 Factors Affecting Percutaneous Absorption

4.6   Process Parameters and Formulation

    4.6.1 Ointment Bases

    4.6.2 Penetration Enhancers

4.7   Method of Preparation

4.8   Manufacturing of Semisolids

4.9   Gels

4.10 Gelling Agents

4.11 Preparation and Packaging

4.12 Evaluation of Semisolids

    4.12.1 Particle Size Distribution

    4.12.2 Skin Irritation Tests

    4.12.3 Measurement of Skin Absorption

4.13 Labelling and Plant Layout

4.1 INTRODUCTION

Semisolid dosage forms are traditionally used for treating topical ailments. The vast majority of them are meant for skin applications. They are also used for treating ophthalmic, nasal, buccal, rectal and vaginal ailments. Drugs incorporated into semisolids either show their activity on the surface layers of tissues or penetrate into internal layers to reach the site of action. Systemic entry of drugs from these products is limited due to various physicochemical properties of dosage forms and biological factors. The barrier nature of most surface biological layers such as skin, cornea and conjunctiva of the eye, and mucosa of nose, mouth, rectum and vagina greatly limits their entry into the systemic circulation. Ointments are semisolid preparations intended for topical application. They are used to provide protective and emollient effects on the skin or carry medicaments for treating certain topical ailments. They are also used to deliver drugs into eye, nose, vagina, and rectum. Creams are basically ointments which are made less greasy by incorporation of water. Presence of water in creams makes them act as emulsions and therefore is sometimes referred as semisolid emulsions. Hydrophilic creams contain large amounts of water in their external phase (e.g., vanishing cream) and hydrophobic creams contain water in the internal phase (e.g., cold cream). An emulsifying agent is used to disperse the aqueous phase in the oily phase or vice versa. As with ointments, creams are formulated to provide protective, emollient actions or deliver drugs to surface or interior layers of skin, rectum and vagina. Creams are softer than ointments and are preferred because of their easy removal from containers and good spreadability over the absorption site.

4.2 ANATOMY AND PHYSIOLOGY OF THE SKIN

The skin is the largest organ of the body and acts as a protective barrier with sensory and immunological functions. Human skin is, on an average, 0.5 mm thick (ranging from 0.05 mm in eye lid to 2 mm). Classification of skin is based on the epidermis alone especially, the surface layer (stratum corneum).

- thick: palms of hand, soles of feet
- thin: rest of the body

Although the skin is one of the major sites for noninvasive delivery of therapeutic agents into the body, this task can be relatively challenging owing to the impermeability of the skin.

4.2.1 Layers of the Skin

Table 4.1 : Layers of the Skin

Skin layer	Description
Epidermis	The external layer mainly composed of layers of keratinocytes but also containing melanocytes, Langerhans cells and Merkel cells.
Basement membrane	The multilayered structure forming the dermoepidermal junction.
Dermis	The area of supportive connective tissue between the epidermis and the underlying subcutis: contains sweat glands, hair roots, nervous cells and fibres, blood and lymph vessels.
Subcutis	The layer of loose connective tissue and fat beneath the dermis.

(1) Epidermis

The epidermis is the outer layer, serving as the physical and chemical barrier between the interior body and exterior environment; the dermis is the deeper layer providing the structural support of the skin, below which is a loose connective tissue layer, the subcutis or hypodermis which is an important depot of fat. The epidermis is stratified squamous epithelium. The main cells of the epidermis are the keratinocytes, which synthesize the protein keratin. Protein bridges called desmosomes connect the keratinocytes, which are in a constant state of transition from the deeper layers to the superficial. The epidermis varies in thickness from 0.05 mm on the eyelids to 0.8-1.5 mm on the soles of the feet and palms of the hand. Moving from the lower layers upwards to the surface, the four layers of the epidermis are:

- stratum basale (basal or germinativum cell layer)
- stratum spinosum (spinous or prickle cell layer)
- stratum granulosum (granular cell layer)
- stratum corneum (horny layer)

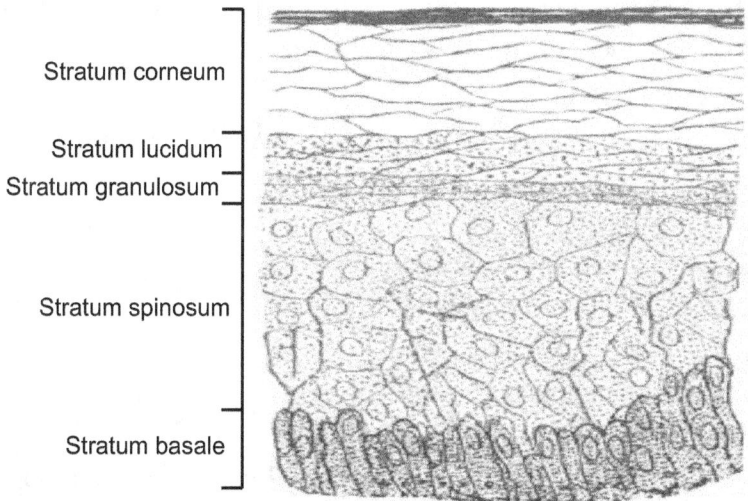

Fig. 4.1: Layers of Epidermis

(2) Basement Membrane

This is a complex structure composed of two layers. The structure is highly irregular with dermal papillae from the papillary dermis projecting perpendicular to the skin surface. The dermo-epidermal junction flattens during ageing which accounts in part for some of the visual signs of ageing.

(3) Dermis

The dermis varies in thickness, ranging from 0.6 mm on the eyelids to 3 mm on the back, palms and soles. It is found below the epidermis and is composed of a tough, supportive cell matrix. Two layers comprise the dermis:

- a thin papillary layer
- a thicker reticular layer.

(4) Subcutis

This is made up of loose connective tissue and fat which can be upto 3 cm thick on the abdomen.

(5) Skin Appendages

There are three main appendages,

- **(A) Hair Follicles:** found all over the body except load bearing areas (soles of feet and palms of hands) and lips.
- **(B) Sebaceous Glands:** secret sebum (mixture of fatty acids and waxes) which help to lubricate skin surface and maintain surface pH of around 5.
- **(C) Sweat Gland:** Eccrine glands at density of 100-200 per cm^2 and apocrine glands less in number and limited to certain area of the skin, for example armpit, nipples and per anal region.

4.2.2 Functions of the Skin

1. Provides a protective barrier against mechanical, thermal and physical injury and noxious agents.
2. Prevents loss of moisture.
3. Reduces harmful effects of UV radiation.
4. Acts as a sensory organ.
5. Helps to regulate temperature control.
6. Plays a role in immunological surveillance.
7. Synthesizes vitamin D_3 (cholecalciferol).

Semisolid dosage forms are products of semisolid consistency and applied to skin or mucous membranes for therapeutic or protective action or cosmetic purpose. Semisolid dosage forms for dermatological drug therapy are intended to produce desired therapeutic action at specific sites in the epidermal tissue. Ability of drug to penetrate the epidermis, dermis and subcutaneous fat layers will lead to transdermal (percutaneous) drug delivery giving rise to systemic action. Therefore, the extents the drug can travel through the different skin layers determine the delivery system. Drugs can penetrate skin barrier by three routes as given below.

- Transcellular (across cells)
- Intercellular (between cells)

Trans appendageal (via hair follicles, sweat and sebum glands)

Percutaneous drug absorption results from direct penetration through the stratum corneum, followed by passing through the epidermal tissues and into the dermis.

(1) across the continuous stratum corneum;

(2) through the hair follicles with their associated sebaceous glands

(3) via the sweat duct.

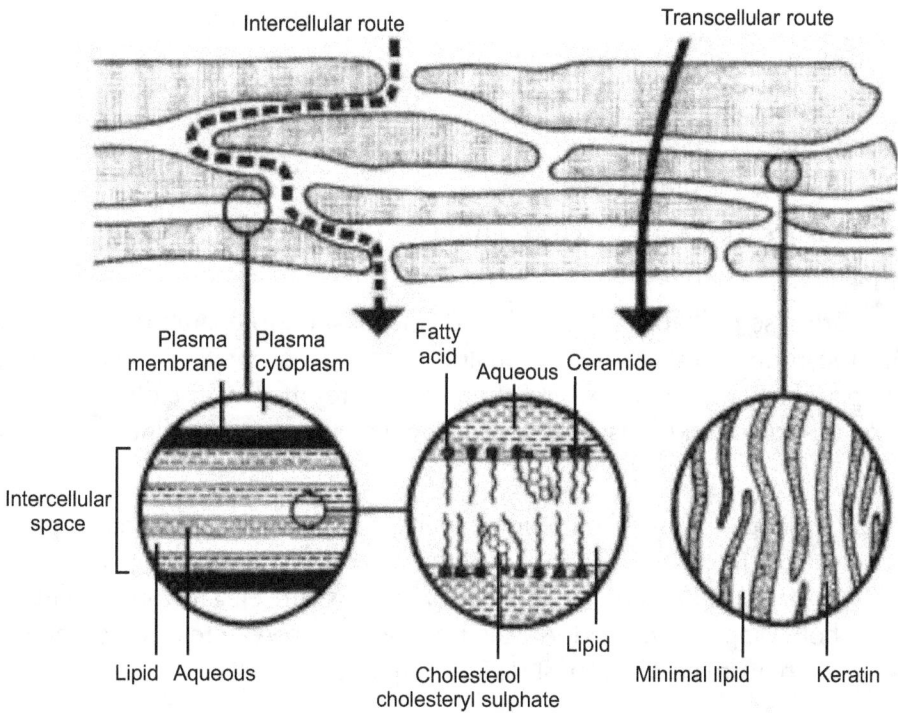

Fig. 4.2: Trans-Cellular Pathway and Inter-Cellular Pathway

4.3 IDEAL PROPERTIES OF SEMISOLID DOSAGE FORMS

(I) Physical Properties

    (a) Smooth texture

    (b) Elegant in appearance

    (c) Non dehydrating

    (d) Non gritty

    (e) Non greasy and non staining

    (f) Non hygroscopic

(II) Physiological Properties

    (a) Non irritating

    (b) Do not alter membrane / skin functioning

    (c) Miscible with skin secretion

    (d) Have low sensitization effect

(III) Application Properties

    (a) Easily applicable with efficient drug release

    (b) High aqueous washability

4.3.1 Ideal Molecular Properties for Drug Penetration

    (a) A low molecular weight (generally less than 600 Daltons).

    (b) An adequate solubility in oil and water.

    (c) A balanced partition coefficient.

    (d) A low melting point.

    (e) Potent drug (maximum 50 mg/day).

4.4 TYPES OF CONVENTIONAL SEMISOLID DOSAGE FORMS

(A) Ointments

They are soft hydrocarbon based semisolid preparations, composed of fluid hydrocarbon meshed in a matrix of higher melting solid hydrocarbon, example: petrolactum. Since they are of greasy nature, they stain cloths. Generally poor solvent for most drugs and usually decrease the drug delivery capabilities of the system.

(B) Creams

They are viscous semisolid emulsion system with opaque appearance compared with the translucent ointments. Consistency and rheological characters depend on whether the cream is w/o or o/w. Properly designed o/w creams are elegant drug delivery system, pleasing in both, appearance and feel after application. O/W creams are non-greasy and are washable. They are good for most topical purposes.

(C) Pastes

Pastes are basically ointments into which a high percentage of insoluble solid has been added. The extraordinary amount of particulate matter stiffens the system. Pastes are less penetrating than ointment. Paste make particularly good protective barrier when placed on the skin, in addition to forming an unbroken film, the solid they contain can absorb and thereby neutralize certain noxious chemicals before they ever reach the skin. Like ointments, paste forms an unbroken relatively, water impermeable film. Unlike ointments, the film is opaque and therefore, an effective sun block accordingly.

(D) Gels (Jellies)

Gels are semisolid coherent system in which a liquid phase is constrained within a polymeric matrix (consisting of natural or synthetic gum) having a high degree of physical or chemical cross-linking. Gels are transparent or translucent non-greasy semisolid gels. Some are as transparent as water itself, an aesthetically pleasing state, other are turbid, as the polymer is present in colloidal aggregates that disperse light. They are used for medication or lubrication.

4.5 PERCUTANEOUS ABSORPTION

The term percutaneous absorption covers the entire process by which a drug applied to the outer surface of the skin is taken up into the systemic circulation. This requires penetration into the layers of the skin with subsequent permeation across each layer and finally uptake into the capillary blood vessels in the upper region of the dermis.

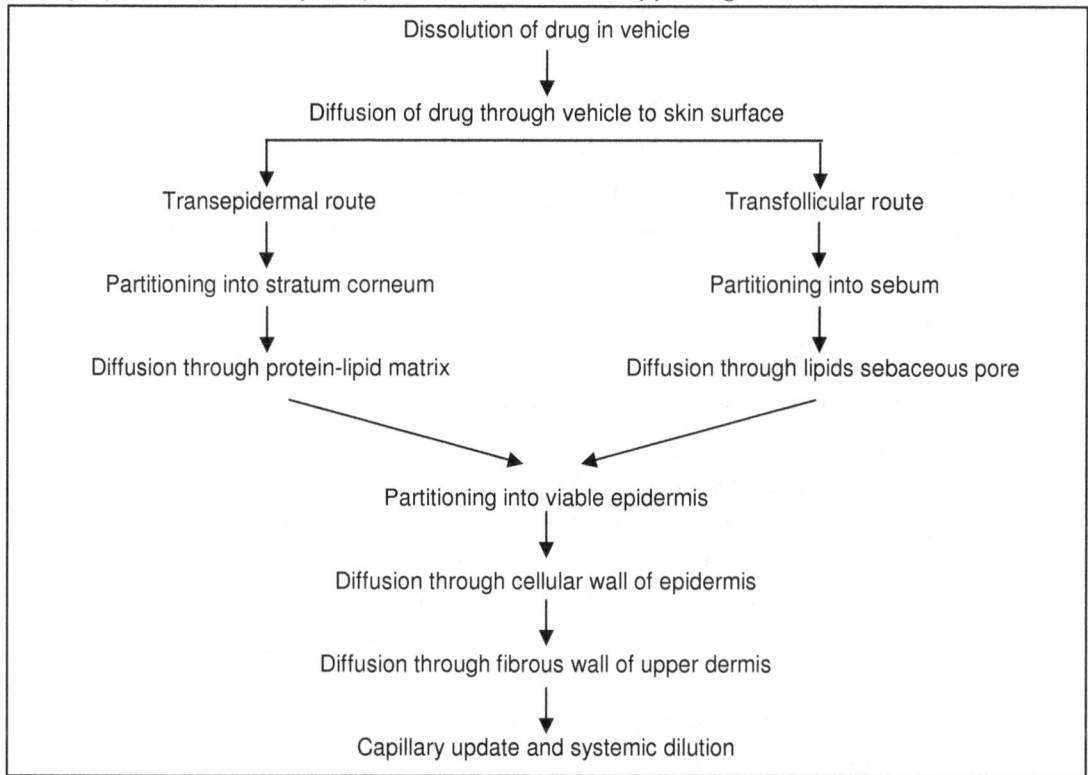

Fig. 4.3: Model of Percutaneous Absorption

The cornified inert layer of epidermis means stratum corneum appears to provide the rate-limiting step to transdermal drug absorption and permeation of the skin depends on diffusion; therefore, the hydration of the skin will affect drug permeability. Absorption via the transdermal route primarily occurs by passive diffusion through stratum corneum. The rate of diffusion is dependent on

- Permeability coefficient of the drug (K_p)
- Applied concentration of the drug (C)
- Surface area of the skin exposed to the drug (A)
- Thickness of the epidermis (h)

Any substance that comes into contact with the skin surface can penetrate the stratum corneum, permeate the skin strata and diffuse into the underlying tissues or become absorbed into the dermal blood supply and hence the systemic circulation.

Regional variations in skin permeability are correlated with quantitative differences in lipid content rather than thickness of stratum corneum. Molecules traverse membranes either by passive diffusion (solute flux is linearly dependent on the solute concentration gradient) or active transport. Percutaneous flux is directly proportional to the concentration gradient and therefore, transport across the skin occurs primarily by passive diffusion. At steady state, the flux due to passive diffusion may be described by Fick's first law,

$$J = k_p \times \Delta a$$

where J = flux of the permeant (moles/cm^2)

k_p = permeability coefficient of the permeant through the membrane (cm/s)

Δa = activity gradient across the membrane (moles/cm^3)

k_p is the inverse of the "resistance", which the membrane offers to solute transport and is defined by,

$$k_p = KD / h$$

where K = membrane-aqueous phase partition coefficient of the solute

D = diffusion coefficient of the solute in the membrane (cm^2/s)

h = diffusion path length through the membrane

The flux rate is a rate process and equal to (driving force) / (resistance).

The driving force for diffusion is the activity gradient (concentration gradient across the permeability barrier). Molecular flux across the membrane can be determined by the solute's size and lipophilicity, if the driving force remains the same. Octanol/water partition coefficient ($\frac{K_o}{K_w}$) has been chosen to be used as the index of lipophilicity.

4.5.1 Factors Affecting Percutaneous Absorption

(I) Biological Factors

1. Skin Condition

The intact, healthy skin is a tough barrier but many agents can damage it. Vesicants such as acids and alkalis injure barrier cells and thereby promote penetration, as do cuts, abrasion and dermatitis. Many solvents open up the complex dense structure of horny layer. Mixtures of non-polar and polar solvents, such as chloroform, methanol removes lipid fraction, forming shunts through which molecules pass more easily. Diseases commonly alter skin condition, so elementary understanding of changes in skin is considered i.e. skin is inflamed with loss of stratum corneum and altered keratinization. In diseases characterized by defective stratum corneum, percutaneous absorption usually increases.

2. Skin Age

It is often assumed that skin of young and elders is more permeable than adult, but there is little evidence for any dramatic difference. Children are more susceptible to the toxic effects of drugs and chemicals, partly because of their greater surface area per unit body weight, thus potent topical steroids, boric acids have produced severe side-effects and death. Premature infants may be born with no stratum corneum.

3. Blood Flow

Theoretically, changes in peripheral circulation could affect transdermal absorption; an increased blood flow could reduce the amount of time a penetrant remains in the dermis and also raise concentration gradient across the skin.

4. Regional Skin Sites

Variations in cutaneous permeability around body depend on the thickness and nature of stratum corneum and the density of skin appendages. However, the absorption rate varies widely for specific substance passing through identical skin sites in different healthy volunteers. The permeability depends on both, the intrinsic resistance to permeation per unit thickness of stratum corneum and overall thickness of tissue. Facial skin in general is more permeable than other body sites.

5. Skin Metabolism

The skin metabolizes steroid, hormones, chemical carcinogens and some drugs. Such metabolism may determine the therapeutic efficacy of topically applied compounds and the carcinogenic response in the skin. It has been estimated that skin can metabolize 5 per cent of topical drugs.

(II) Physicochemical Factors

1. Skin Hydration

When water saturates the skin the tissue swells, softens and wrinkles and its permeability increases markedly. Hydration of stratum corneum is one of the most important factors in increasing penetration rate of most substances that permeate skin. Hydration may result from water diffusing from underlying epidermal layers or from perspiration that accumulates after application of occlusive vehicle or dressing.

2. Temperature and pH

The penetration rate of material through human skin can change tenfold for large temperature variation, as the diffusion coefficient decreases as the temperature falls. Only unionized molecule pass readily across lipid membrane. Thus proportion of unionized drug in the applied phase mainly determines the effective membrane gradient and this fraction depends on pH. The stratum corneum is remarkably resistant to alteration in pH, tolerating a range of 3-9.

3. Drug Concentration

The flux of solute is proportional to the concentration gradient across the entire barrier phase. One requirement for maximal flux in a thermodynamically stable situation is that donor solution should be saturated. The concentration differential is usually considered to be driving force for diffusion.

4. Partition Coefficient

The partition coefficient is important in establishing the flux of drug through stratum corneum. The stratum corneum to vehicle partition coefficient is then crucially important in establishing high initial concentration of diffusant in the first layer of membrane.

4.6 PROCESS PARAMETERS AND FORMULATION

The most common semi-solid dosage formulations are therapeutic creams, ointments, gels, lotions, emulsions, salves, pastes and other forms of similar viscous consistency. Topical and ophthalmic are the primary routes of administration for semisolids. Semisolid drug products, depending on their use, can be sterile or nonsterile. Creams/ointments typically contain one or more drug substances dissolved or dispersed in aqueous, oil or a suitable base. Creams possess a fluid consistency and have traditionally been called oil-in-water or water-in-oil emulsions. They could be dispersions of long-chain fatty acids or alcohols that are water washable or miscible. Some common manufacturing processes are mixing, heating/cooling, dispersion/homogenization, deaeration, transfer and other techniques for these viscous substances. Filling and packaging is typically into single-or multiple-unit containers such as rigid bottles or jars, collapsible tubes or flexible pouches.

Formulation of Ointments

Ingredients used for formulating semisolids include, bases, antimicrobial preservative, humectants, fragrances, emulsifier, gelling agent and permeation enhancer.

4.6.1 Ointment Bases

Semisolid bases do not only act as carriers of the medicaments, but they also control the extent of absorption of medicaments incorporated. An ointment base should be compatible with skin, stable, smooth, non-irritating, non-sensitizing, inert and should release incorporated medicament, readily. A base for ophthalmic semisolids must be non-irritating to the eye and it should also be sterilizable conveniently.

Selection of ointment base depends on the following factors:

- Desired release rate of the drug substance from the ointment base.
- Rate and extent of topical or percutaneous drug absorption.
- Desirability of occlusion of moisture from skin.
- Stability of the drug in the ointment base.
- Easy removal of base on washing.
- Characteristic of the surface to which it is applied.

Bases are classified based on their composition and physical characteristics. The U.S. Pharmacopeia (USP) classifies ointment bases as hydrocarbon bases (oleaginous bases), absorption bases, water - removable bases and water - soluble bases (water - miscible bases).

(I) Hydrocarbon bases are made of oleaginous materials. They provide emollient and protective properties and remain in the skin for prolonged periods. It is difficult to incorporate aqueous phases into hydrocarbon bases. Petrolatum USP, white petrolatum USP, yellow ointment USP, and white ointment USP are examples of hydrocarbon bases.

(II) Absorption bases contain small amounts of water. They provide relatively less emollient properties than hydrocarbon bases. Similar to hydrocarbon bases, absorption bases are also difficult to remove from the skin due to their hydrophobic nature. Hydrophilic petrolatum USP and lanolin USP are examples of absorption bases.

(III) Water-removable bases are basically oil-in-water emulsions. Unlike hydrocarbon and absorption bases, a large proportion of aqueous phase can be incorporated into water - removable bases with the aid of suitable emulsifying agents. It is easy to remove these bases from the skin due to their hydrophilic nature. Hydrophilic ointment USP is an example of water removable ointment base.

(IV) Water-soluble bases do not contain any oily or oleaginous phase. Solids can be easily incorporated into these bases. They may be completely removed from the skin due to their water solubility.

Some Compendial Bases Used in Ointments and Creams

- **Lanolin:** Lanolin is a refined, decolorized, and deodorized material obtained from sheep wool. It is available as a pale yellow, waxy material with a characteristic odor. It is extensively used in the preparation of hydrophobic ointments and water - in - oil creams. As lanolin is prone to oxidation, antioxidants such as butylated hydroxytoluene are generally included. Although lanolin is insoluble in water, it is miscible with water upto 1:2 ratios.

- **Hydrous lanolin:** Incorporation of about 25 - 30% of water into lanolin gives hydrous lanolin. Gradual addition of water into molten lanolin with constant stirring helps in water incorporation. It is available as a pale yellow, oily material with a characteristic odor. The water uptake capacity of hydrous lanolin is higher than lanolin, and it is used for preparing topical hydrophobic ointments or water - in - oil creams with larger aqueous phase.

- **Lanolin alcohols:** Lanolin alcohol is prepared from lanolin by the saponification process and is used as a hydrophobic vehicle in pharmaceutical ointments and creams. It is available as a brittle solid material pale yellow in color with a faint characteristic odor. The brittle powder becomes plastic under warm conditions. It is practically insoluble in water and soluble in boiling ethanol. Lanolin alcohol possesses emollient properties, which make it suitable for preparing dry - skin ointments, eye ointments, and water - in - oil creams.

- **Petrolatum:** Petrolatum is also known as yellow soft paraffin. It is an inert material obtained from petroleum, which contains branched and unbranched hydrocarbons.

It is available as soft oily material and appears pale yellow to yellow in color. Concentrations upto 30% are used in creams. Petrolatum shows phase transitions on heating to about 35°C.

- **Petrolatum and lanolin alcohols:** Various quantities of lanolin alcohols are mixed with petrolatum to form these mixtures. Wool ointment British Pharmacopoeia (BP) 2001 contains 6% lanolin alcohols and 10% petrolatum. These proportions can be varied to alter physical properties such as consistency and melting range. They are available as soft solids pale ivory in color and possess a characteristic odor. These mixtures are insoluble in water and concentrations ranging 5 – 50% are used for preparing hydrophobic ointments. They are also used for preparing water - in - oil emollient creams.

- **Paraffins:** Paraffins are obtained by distillation of crude petroleum followed by purification processes. The purified fraction contains saturated hydrocarbons. Paraffins are insoluble in water and is generally used to prepare hydrophobic topical ointments and water - in - oil creams. Repeated heating and congealing are avoided during formulation as they change the physical properties of paraffin.

- **PEGs:** PEGs are hydrophilic materials and are extensively used in the preparation of hydrophilic ointments and creams. They are non-irritants and are easily washed from skin surfaces. Products with varying consistency are prepared by mixing different grades of PEGs.

- **Stearic acid:** Stearic acid is obtained by hydrolysis of fat or hydrogenation of vegetable oils. Compendial stearic acid contains a mixture of stearic acid and palmitic acids. It is available as powder or crystalline solid which is white to yellowish white in color and possesses a characteristic odor. Although stearic acid is insoluble in water, partially neutralized grades form a cream base when combined with about 10 times its weight of aqueous solvents. Concentrations upto 20% are used for formulating creams and ointments.

- **Carnauba wax:** Carnauba wax contains a mixture of esters of acids and hydroxy acids isolated from Brazilian carnauba palm. It also contains various resins, hydrocarbons, acids, polyhydric alcohols and water.

- **Cetyl alcohol:** Cetyl alcohol is obtained by hydrogenolysis or esterification of fatty acids and contains not less than 90% cetyl alcohol along with other aliphatic alcohols. It is available as flakes or granules white in color and possesses a characteristic odor. Concentrations ranging from 2 to 10% are used in topical preparations to impart emollient, emulsifying, water - absorptive and stiffening properties. Mixtures of petrolatum and cetyl alcohol are sometimes used for preparing creams.

- **Emulsifying wax:** Emulsifying wax, also known as anionic emulsifying wax, is a mixture of cetostearyl alcohol, sodium lauryl sulfate, and purified water.

Emulsifying wax BP contains about 90% cetostearyl alcohol, 10% sodium lauryl sulfate, and 4% purified water. Although emulsifying wax is insoluble in water, its emulsifying properties help in preparing hydrophilic oil - in - water emulsions. Ointment bases are prepared by mixing upto 50% emulsifying wax with liquid or soft paraffins. At concentrations upto 10%, it forms creams.

- **White bees wax:** White wax is a bleached form of yellow wax which is usually obtained from the honeycomb of bees and hence is known as bleached wax or white bees wax. It contains about 70% esters of straight - chain monohydric alcohols, 15% free acids, 12% carbohydrates, and 1% free wax alcohols and stearic esters of fatty acids. It is available as granules or sheets which are white in color and possesses a characteristic odor. White wax is insoluble in water and melts between 61 and 65 ° C.

- **Yellow bees wax:** Is obtained from honey combs. It contains about 70% esters of straight - chain monohydric alcohols, 15% free acids, 12% carbohydrates and 1% free wax alcohols and stearic esters of fatty acids. It is available as noncrystalline pieces which are yellow in color and possesses a characteristic odor. It is practically insoluble in water and melts at 61 - 65 °C. It is used in the preparation of hydrophobic ointments and water - in - oil creams because of its viscosity enhancing properties. Concentrations upto 20% are used for producing ointments and creams.

Table 4.2 : Bases Used in Ointments/Creams

Name	Melting Range
Carnauba wax	80 - 88°C
Cetyl alcohol	47 - 53°C
Cetyl ester wax	43 - 47°C
Hydrous lanolin	38 - 44°C
Lanolin	38 - 44 °C
Lanolin alcohols	> 56°C
Microcrystalline wax	54 - 102°C
Paraffin	47 - 65°C
Petrolatum	38 - 60°C
Yellow wax	61 - 65°C
White wax	62 - 65°C
Stearyl alcohol	55 - 60°C
Stearic acid	> 54°C

4.6.2 Penetration Enhancers

Penetration enhancer acts by four different mechanisms as given below.

1. By increasing the diffusion coefficient of the drug.
2. By increasing the effective concentration of the drug in the vehicle.
3. By improving partitioning between the formulation and the stratum corneum.
4. By decreasing the skin thickness.

Examples of penetration enhancers are,

1. Surfactants: (a) Ionic: SLS, Na laureate, etc. (b) Non ionic: Tween 80, Polysorbates, etc.
2. Bile salts and derivatives: Na glyacolate, Na deoxycholate, etc.
3. Fatty acid and derivatives: Oleic acid, Caprylic acid, etc.
4. Chelating agents: EDTA, Citric acid, etc.
5. Sulphoxide: DMSO, DMA, DMF, etc.
6. Polyols: PG, PEG, Glycerol, etc.
7. Monohydric alcohols: Ethanol, 2-Propanol, etc.
8. Miscellaneous: (a) Urea and its derivatives, (b) Terpenes and Terpenoids, (c) Phospholipids, (d) Water.

Table 4.3 : Formulation Components for Topical Drug Products

Component Functionality	Component Description	Examples
Emollient/stiffening agent/ointment base	Main structure-forming materials for semisolid dosage form	Carnauba wax, Cetyl alcohol, Cetyl ester wax, Emulsifying wax, Hydrous lanolin, Lanolin, Lanolin alcohols, Microcrystalline wax, Paraffin, Petrolatum, Polyethylene glycol, Stearic acid, Stearyl alcohol, White wax, Yellow wax.
	Based on their composition and physical characteristics, the USP classifies ointment bases as hydrocarbon bases (oleaginous bases), absorption bases, water-removable bases, and water-soluble bases.	
Emulsifying agent/solubilizing agent	Surfactants used to reduce the interfacial tension to stabilize emulsions and to improve the wetting and	Polysorbate 20, Polysorbate 80, Polysorbate 60, Poloxamer, Emulsifying wax, Sorbitan monostearate, Sorbitan

Component Functionality	Component Description	Examples
	solubility of hydrophobic materials	monooleate, Sodium lauryl sulfate, Propylene glycol monostearate, Diethylene glycol monoethyl ether, Docusate sodium.
Humectant (polyols)	Promotes the retention of water in the system	Glycerine, Propylene glycol, Polyethylene glycol, Sorbitol solution, 1,2,6 Hexanetriol.
Thickening/Gelling agent	Increases viscosity	Carbomer, Methyl cellulose, Sodium carboxyl methyl cellulose, Carrageenan, Colloidal silicon dioxide, Guar gum, Hydroxypropyl cellulose, Hydroxypropyl methyl cellulose, Gelatin, Polyethylene oxide, Alginic acid, Sodium alginate, Fumed silica.
	Main structure-forming materials for gels	
Preservative	Prevents microbial growth	Benzoic acid, Propyl paraben, Methyl paraben, Imidurea, Sorbic acid, Potassium sorbate, Benzalkonium chloride, Phenyl mercuric acetate, Chlorobutanol, Phenoxyethanol.
Permeation enhancer	Increases the permeation by promoting the diffusion, partitioning, or the drug solubility of an active ingredient through the stratum corneum	Propylene glycol, Ethanol, Isopropyl alcohol, Oleic acid, Polyethylene glycol.
Chelating agent	Binds metal ions to minimize metal-catalyzed degradation and to enhance the preservative effect	Ethylene diamine tetraacetate.

Component Functionality	Component Description	Examples
Antioxidant	To minimize oxidative deterioration	Butylated hydroxyanisole, Butylated hydroxytoluene.
Acidifying/alkalizing /buffering agent	Maintain a proper pH for the dosage form	Citric acid, Phosphoric acid, Sodium hydroxide, Monobasic sodium phosphate, Triethyl amine.
Vehicle/solvent	Facilitate the dispersion and/or dissolution of API.	Purified water, Hexylene glycol, Propylene glycol, Oleyl alcohol, Propylene carbonate, Mineral oil.

Many excipients used in topical drug products have dual or multiple functionalities.

Table 4.4 : Designing of Semisolid Dosage Forms

Area	Consideration	Comments
Drug substance	Quality of API and adequate DMF (Drug Master File)	The selection of an API source is a central part of generic drug formulation development. Pay attention to the impurities which are not present in the RLD (Reference Listed Drug) and residual solvents which are not listed in the ICH Q3C.
	Residual solvents	
	Physical state of API, e.g., melting point (liquid, low melting point, or high melting drug), micronized drug, polymorphs, etc.	Preformulation data are critical for generic formulation and process development. This data may include APIs physical state, particle size, morphic form, solubility properties, sensitivity to light, moisture or air, and degradation pathway.
	Solubility of API in hydrophobic and hydrophilic vehicles	
	Cost and availability issue	
Excipients	Compendial material versus non-compendial material	Compendial excipients usually are preferred; non-compendial materials are acceptable with justifications.
	Residual solvents	The film is required to provide residual solvent data and test specifications to demonstrate that its drug product is in compliance with USP requirements.

Area	Consideration	Comments
	Physical state of excipients, e.g., melting point (liquid, low melting point, or high melting excipient)	Excipient compatibility study using a binary mixture is desired to ensure the drug product stability prior to the drug product development. However, in many cases, homogeneous mixing of the selected excipient and the API is impossible. Different excipient compatibility study design can be used.
	Excipient compatibility	Generally, the excipients used in the RLD are presumed compatible with the drug substance. The formulator should be aware that different vendors or grades may contain different impurities, which in turn may trigger the drug degradation.
	Hydrophilic–lipophilic balance (HLB) and type of emulsifier	It is prudent to keep the type of emulsifier(s), hydrophilic–lipophilic balance (HLB) of emulsifier and solvent to emulsifier ratio similar to those of the RLD, if the test formula is different from the RLD.
	Functionality	Excipients used in topical formulation can have emollient and hydrating effects and make the skin softer smoother, and firmer.
Physicochemical properties of drug product	Target product profile such as dosage form, viscosity, pH, strength, release profile, in vitro permeation rate, homogeneity, etc.	Characterization of the RLD in terms of product attributes and stability profile is essential for the generic drug development.
		Quality target product profile and critical quality attributes need to be identified as a part of quality by design.
Container closure system	Selection of container closure system as close to that of the RLD as possible.	Material of construct for the selected container closure system should be similar to that of the RLD. It is prudent to conduct a preliminary stability study using the final formula to demonstrate package compatibility in the formulation development stage.
	Package compatibility	

Area	Consideration	Comments
Chemical stability	Consistency for chemical properties of the drug product over time	The goal, if possible is to maintain assay value as close to 100% label claim and impurity level as close to 0% throughout the shelf-life period.
Physical stability	Consistency for physical properties of the drug product over time	The goal, if possible is to maintain physical properties of the drug product throughout the shelf-life period. Potential problems include separation of phases, syneresis, pH change, specific gravity change, viscosity change, homogeneity of dosage form, etc.
Manufacturability and scalability	Process equipment	Appropriate process equipment and process parameters need to be identified as a part of quality by design.
	Process parameters, such as agitation rate, mixing time, temperature, etc.	
		Based on the past scale-up experience of the same type of formulation and process as well as engineering principles, the commercial size scale up, and equipment changes should be justified.
Preservative efficacy	Selection of preservatives	The minimum acceptable limit of preservatives in a drug product must be demonstrated by performing a microbial challenge assay as specified in USP.
	Optimization of preservative concentration	
	Minimum acceptable limit of preservatives	
Patient's acceptance	Consistency of the preparation	Patient's acceptance is the key for a successful drug product commercialization in a competitive marketplace. A test panel evaluating the consistency, washability, cosmetic feel, and rub-in properties of topical drug products can be used to identify a commercially viable drug product.
	Sensory perception before, during and after application	

4.7 METHOD OF PREPARATION OF OINTMENTS (SMALL SCALE)

1. Trituration Method

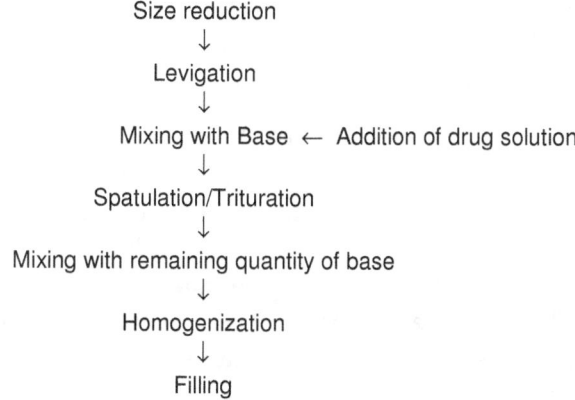

Size reduction
↓
Levigation
↓
Mixing with Base ← Addition of drug solution
↓
Spatulation/Trituration
↓
Mixing with remaining quantity of base
↓
Homogenization
↓
Filling

Fig. 4.4 : Steps in Preparation of Ointment

2. Fusion Method

For small scale, fusion method, porcelain dish is used to melt high melting point components first. Then low melting components should be added and mix with continuous stirring (means decreasing order of melting point). Drug is added to above mixture with continuous stirring and allows cooling. Liquid components if any should be added usually at 40°C to above molten mass. Precautions should be taken to avoid premature cooling to avoid grittiness in the final product. Heat labile substances added last, when the temperature of the mixture is low enough not to cause decomposition of the ingredients. Finally formulation may be subjected to further homogenization to get more uniform and smooth product.

A wide range of machines are available for the large scale production of ointments and creams. Each of these machines is designed to perform certain unit operations, such as milling, separation, mixing, emulsification and deaeration. Milling is performed to reduce the size of actives and other additives. Various fluid energy mills, impact mills, cutter mills, compression mills, screening mills and tumbling mills are used for this purpose. Separators are employed for separating materials of different size, shape and densities. Either centrifugal separators or vibratory shakers are used for separation. Mixing of the actives and other formulation components with the ointment or cream base is performed using various types of low shear mixers, high shear mixers, roller mills and static mixers. Mixers with heating provisions are also used to aid in the melting of bases and mixing of components. Entrapment of air into the final product due to mixing processes is a common issue. Effective deaeration is generally achieved by using vacuum vessel deaerators. Various low and high shear shifters are used to transfer materials from the production vessel to the packaging machines. In the packaging area, various types of holders (e.g., pneumatic, gravity, and auger holders), fillers (e.g., piston, peristaltic pump, gear pump, orifice and auger fillers), and sealers (e.g., heat, torque, microwave, indication, and mechanical crimping sealers) are used to complete the unit operations.

Creams are produced with the help of low shear and high shear emulsifiers. These emulsifiers are used to disperse the hydrophilic components in the hydrophobic dispersion phase (e.g., water – in – oil creams) or oleaginous materials in aqueous dispersion medium (oil – in – water creams).

4.8 MANUFACTURING OF SEMISOLIDS

1. Preparation of Oil and Aqueous Phase

The components of oil or fat mixture are usually placed into a stainless steel steam-jacketed kettle, melted and mixed. Transfer of large quantities of petroleum is expedited by heating the petroleum in the steel drum. Then drums should be placed in a hot room (60-62°C) until the petrolatum is fluid. The liquefied petrolatum can then be transferred to mixing kettle. The oil phase is transferred by gravity or pump to the emulsion mixing kettle whose walls have been heated to temperature of oil phase to prevent some of its higher melting components from congealing. The components of aqueous phase are then should be dissolved in purified water and filtered.

2. Mixing of Phase

The phases are usually mixed at a temperature of 70-72°C because, at this temperature intimate mixing of the liquid phase can occur. Decreasing the temperature at which the phase is mixed decreases the cooling time. The properties of some emulsion depend on the temperature at which the phases are mixed. The initial mixing temperature must be raised above 70-72 °C. The phase can be mixed in one of three ways as given below:

    I.   Simultaneous blending of phases

    II. Addition of discontinuous phase to continuous phase

    III. Addition of continuous phase to discontinuous phase

The third process is preferred for many emulsion systems since the emulsion undergoes an inversion of the emulsion type during the addition of continuous phase, which results in a finer phase globule.

(a) Planetary Motion Mixers

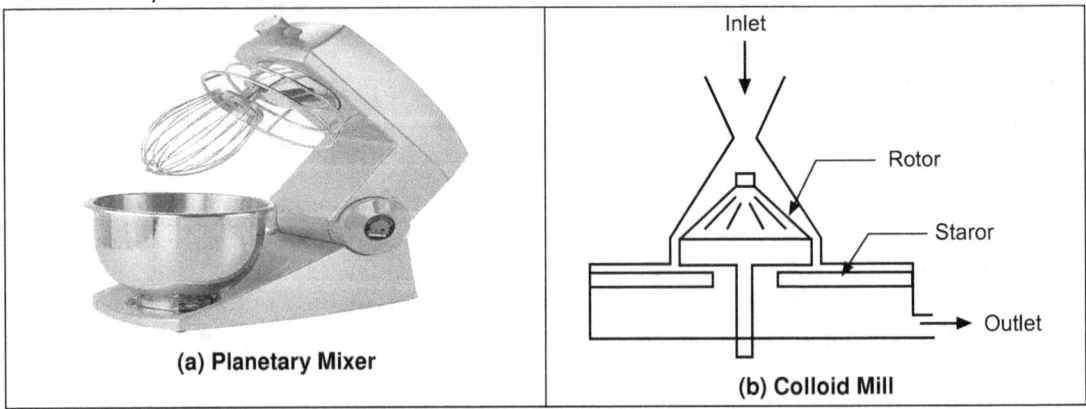

(a) Planetary Mixer

(b) Colloid Mill

Fig. 4.5 : Planetary Motion Mixers

For mixing of semi-solid ingredients mainly planetary mixer is used. For reduction of semi-solid ingredients mainly colloid mill is used. Colloid Mill is suitable for homogenizing, emulsifying, dispersing, mixing. During movement of rotor (3000-20000 rpm), centrifugal force throws a part of the dispersion on to the stator.

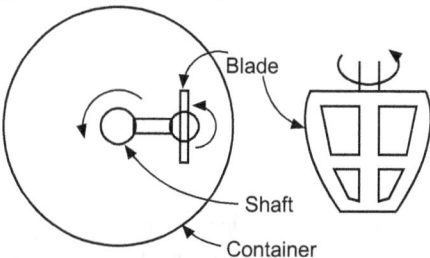

Fig. 4.6 : Planetary Motion Mixer

It consists of a circular base. Inside the container a blade rotates around its own axis. The axis of the blade again rotates along a shaft. Thus the motion of the blade is similar to the motion of a planet around the sun. The planet is rotating along its own axis and at the same time the planet is rotating around the sun. There is very little clearance between the blade and the wall of the container. This design allows the revolving blade to handle (mix) a small amount of mass at a time. Again the blade is moving, carrying the mass to other places. The blade is scraping the materials those are sticking to the wall of the container.

(b) Sigma Blender

It uses two mixer blades, the shape of which resembles the Greek letter "sigma" (Σ). The two blades rotate towards each other and operate in a mixing vessel which has a double trough shape, each blade fitting into a trough. The two blades rotate at different speeds, one usually about twice the speed of the other, resulting in a lateral pulling of the material and divisions into two troughs, while the blade shape and difference in speed causes end-to-end movement.

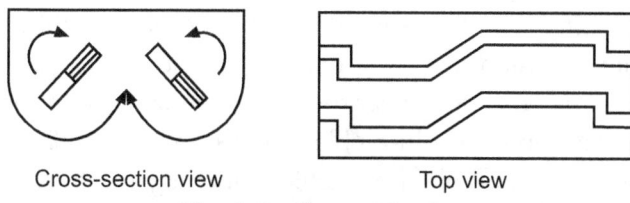

Cross-section view   Top view

Fig. 4.7 : Sigma Blender

Applications

- These types of mixers are of sturdy construction and high power, hence, they can handle even the heaviest plastic materials and products like tablet granule and ointments.

- To reduce the entrainment of air in ointment masses the sigma mixer can be enclosed and operated under reduced pressure, which is an excellent method for avoiding entrainment of air and may assist in minimizing decomposition of oxidizable materials, but it must be used with caution if mixer contains volatile ingredients.

- As with many other mixers, the vessel is jacketed for heating or cooling and in this case, the blades can be hollow for the same purpose. This can be very useful in practice, since some semi-solids may be reduced in viscosity by heating, while with other materials it may be necessary to dissipate the heat resulting from the energy put into the mixing process.

For semisolid mixing, planetary and sigma blenders are used to mix the ointment base ingredients, solids and liquids. Three roll mill is used in mixing solid particles with ointment base.

(c) Three Roll Mill

Roller mills consist of one or more rollers. Three roll types is preferred for semisolid preparations. The rollers rotate at different speed. The material is to be place in the hopper which then passes through roller B and C. Materials coming into the rollers are crushed, depending on the gap between the rollers.

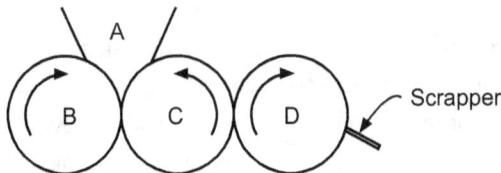

Fig. 4.8 : Cross-section of Three Roll Mill

The gap between C and D (lesser than the previous one) reduces the particles further and smoothes the mixture. A scrapper continuously removes the materials from the roller D. Roller C moves to-and-fro along its axis to give a kneading action.

3. Cooling the Semisolid Emulsion

Following the addition of the phase, the rate of cooling is generally slow to allow for adequate mixing while emulsion is still liquid. Aeration may occur if the semisolid thickens considerably upon cooing and steps should be taken to prevent this. If perfume is to be added to oil in water emulsion, it is best done while the mixture is at a temperature of 43-45°C. The perfume may be added near room temperature to water in oil emulsion. The drug is added in solution form. An insoluble powder should be dispersed in continuous phase prior to removing the semisolid from kettle for homogenization/or storage.

4. Homogenization

The creams or ointments that require further treatment are then transferred to the proper homogenizer. Uniform dispersion of an insoluble drug in a semisolid, as well as reduction of size of fatty aggregates can be attained by the passage of warm ointment or cream through a homogenizer or mill.

5. Storage of Semisolid

It is usual practice to store the semisolid until the specified quality control tests have been completed, before packaging into appropriate containers, tubes, jars or single dose packets. Topical semi-solid dosage forms should be kept in well-closed containers. The preparation should maintain its pharmaceutical integrity throughout shelf-life when stored at the temperature indicated on the label; the temperature should normally not exceed 25°C. Special storage recommendations or limitations are indicated in individual monographs.

Hand Filling

Weighted amount of ointment is to be placed in a jar with the help of flexible spatula then ointment should be forced down to bottom and along walls of jar to avoid air entrapment.

Mechanical Filling

In this method, ointments can be filled in tin jars and polyethylene tubes. Filling is done by pressure filler which consist of nozel and piston from which ointment oozes out on applying pressure on piston tubes, filled from back side and then are sealed. Vacuum fillers are also available in which nozzle is attached to vacuum pump.

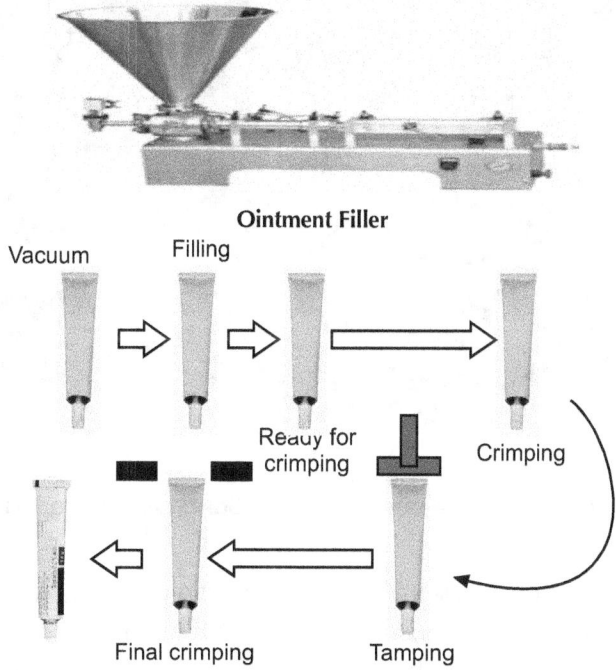

Fig. 4.9 : Ointment Tube Filling Process

Ointment should be stored at cool place to avoid softening and liquification of base and should be labelled as, "FOR EXTERNAL USE ONLY".

Packaging

An ideal container should protect the product from the external atmosphere such as heat, humidity and particulates, be nonreactive with the product components, and be easy to use, light in weight and economic. Aluminium tubes with special internal epoxy coatings are commercially available for improving the compatibility and stability of products. Various modified plastic materials are used for making ointment tubes. Tubes made of low-density polyethylene (LDPE) are generally soft and flexible and offer good moisture protection. Tubes made of high-density polyethylene (HDPE) are relatively harder but offer high moisture protection. Polypropylene containers offer high heat resistance. Plastic containers made of polyethylene terephthalate (PET) are transparent and provide superior chemical compatibility. Ointments meant for ophthalmic, nasal, rectal, and vaginal applications are supplied with special application tips for the ease of product administration. A recent method known as blow fill sealing (BFS) performs fabrication of container, filling of product and sealing operations in a single stage and hence is gaining greater attention.

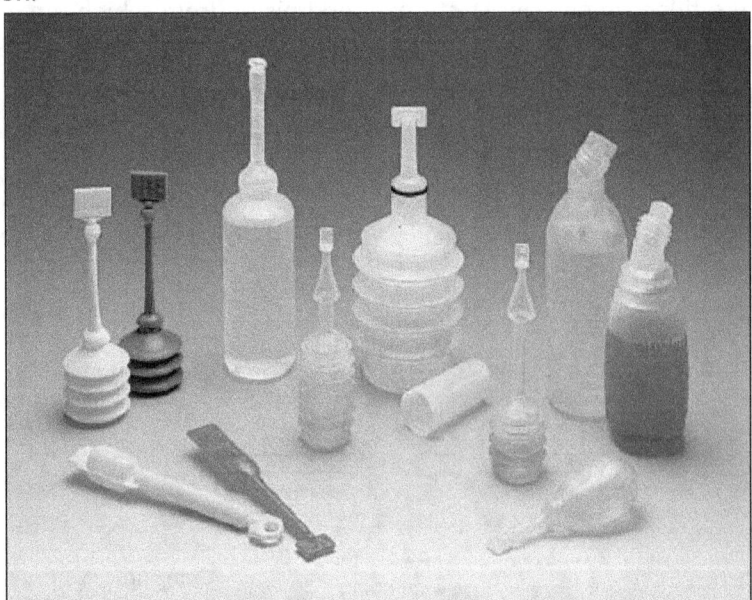

Fig. 4.10 : Containers for Semi-Solid Dosage Forms

4.9 GELS

Gels are attractive delivery systems as they are simple to manufacture and suitable for administering drugs through skin, oral, buccal, ophthalmic, nasal, otic and vaginal routes. They also provide intimate contact between the drug and the site of action or absorption. Gels may appear transparent or turbid based on the type of gelling agent used. They exhibit different physical properties, namely, imbibition, swelling, syneresis and thixotropy. Imbibition refers to the uptake of water or other liquids by gels without any considerable increase in its volume. Swelling refers to the increase in the volume of gel by uptake of water or other liquids. This property of most gels is influenced by temperature, pH, presence of electrolytes and other formulation ingredients. Syneresis refers to the contraction or shrinkage of gels as a result of squeezing out of dispersion medium from the gel matrix. It is due to the excessive stretching of macromolecules and expansion of elastic forces during swelling. Thixotropy refers to the non - Newtonian flow nature of gels, which is characterized by a reversible gel-to-sol formation with no change in volume or temperature.

Gels are classified as hydrogels and organogels based on the physical state of the gelling agent in the dispersion. Hydrogels are prepared with water soluble materials or water dispersible colloids. Organogels are prepared using water insoluble oleaginous materials.

(a) Hydrogels: Natural and synthetic gums such as tragacanth, sodium alginate, and pectin, inorganic materials such as alumina, bentonite, silica, and veegum and organic materials such as cellulose polymers form hydrogels in water.

(b) Organogels: Organogels are also known as oleaginous gels. They are prepared using water insoluble lipids such as glycerol esters of fatty acids, which swell in water and form different types of lyotropic liquid crystals. Widely used glycerol esters of fatty acids include glycerol monooleate, glycerol monopalmito stearete and glycerol monolinoleate. They generally exist as waxes at room temperature and form cubic liquid crystals in water and increase the viscosity of dispersion. Waxes such as carnauba wax, ceresin wax and spermaceti wax are used in cosmetic organogel preparations.

(c) Stimuli Responsive Hydrogels: The three dimensional networks of hydrophilic polymers absorb a large quantity of water and form soft structures which resemble biological tissues. Swelling properties of these hydrogels can be altered by various physicochemical parameters. Physical factors such as temperature, pH, and ionic strength of the swelling medium and chemical factors such as the structure of polymer (linear/branched) and chemical modifications (crosslinking) can be altered to tailor their swelling rate. This feature makes them very attractive for drug delivery and biomedical applications.

4.10 GELLING AGENTS

The following sections briefly describe the source, physicochemical properties and formulation of some Pharmacopeial gelling agents.

(1) Alginic Acid: Alginic acid is tasteless and odorless and occurs as a yellowish white fibrous powder. The main source for this naturally occurring hydrophilic colloidal polysaccharide is different species of brown sea weed, known as Phaeophyceae. It consists of a mixture of d-mannuronic acid and l-glucuronic acids. It is used in gels due to its thickening and swelling properties. Alginic acid is insoluble in water; however, it absorbs 200 - 300 times its own weight of water and swells. The viscosity of alginic acid gels can be altered by changing the molecular weight and concentration.

(2) **Bentonite:** Bentonite is a naturally occurring colloidal hydrated aluminium silicate and contains traces of calcium, magnesium and iron. It is odorless, available as fine crystalline powder and is cream to grayish in color. The particles are negatively charged. Its high water uptake and swelling and thickening properties make it suitable for preparing gels. It swells to about 12 fold when it comes in contact with water. The viscosity of bentonite dispersion increases with increase in concentration. The gel forming properties increase with addition of alkaline materials such as magnesium oxide and decrease with addition of alcohol or electrolytes. Use of hot water and stirring improve wetting and dispersion of bentonite particles in the preparation of the gel.

(3) **Carbomer:** Carbomers are one of the widely used gelling agents in topical preparations due to their extensive swelling properties. They are obtained by cross linking acrylic acid with allyl sucrose or allyl pentaerythritol. Carbomers are generally available as hygroscopic powders, are white in color and possess a characteristic odor. Presence of about 60% carboxylic acid in its composition makes them acidic. Carbomer 934P, 971P, 974P and so on, are used for preparing clear gel. Aqueous dispersions of carbomers are usually low viscous and on neutralization they form high viscous gels.

(4) **Carboxymethylcellulose Calcium (Calcium CMC):** A calcium salt of polycarboxymethyl ether of cellulose, calcium CMC is obtained by carboxymethylation of cellulose and conversion into calcium salt. Different molecular grades are prepared by changing the degree of carboxymethylation. It is available as a fine powder, white to yellowish white in color and hygroscopic in nature. Calcium CMC has swelling and viscosity enhancing properties in water. It can swell twice its volume in water.

(5) **Carboxymethylcellulose Sodium (Sodium CMC):** A sodium salt of polycarboxymethyl ether of cellulose, sodium CMC is obtained by treating alkaline cellulose with sodium monochloroacetate. It is available as white colored granular powder. Although the viscosity of gels is stable over a wide range of pH (4 -10), a fall in pH below 2 or a rise to above 10 results in physical instability and viscosity reduction. Higher viscosity is obtained at neutral pH conditions.

(6) **Ethyl Cellulose:** Ethyl cellulose is a synthetic polymer made of β-anhydroglucose units connected by acetyl linkages. It is obtained by ethylating alkaline cellulose solution with chloroethane. Ethyl cellulose is available as a free flowing powder which is tasteless and white in color. Although it is insoluble in water, it is incorporated into topical preparations due to its viscosity enhancing properties.

(7) **Gelatin:** Gelatin is a protein obtained by acid or alkali hydrolysis of animal tissues that contain large amounts of collagen. Gelatin is available as yellow - colored powder or granules. It swells in water and improves the viscosity of dispersions. Gels can be prepared by dissolving gelatin in hot water and cooling to 35°C. Temperature greatly influences the viscosity and stability of gelatin dispersions. It transforms to a gel at temperatures above 40°C and undergoes depolymerization above 50°C.

(8) Guar Gum: Guar gum is a high molecular weight polysaccharide obtained from the endosperms of guar plant. It mainly contains d - galactan and d - mannan. It is available as powder which is odorless and white to yellowish white in color. It readily disperses in water and forms viscous gels. The viscosity of gel is influenced by the particle size of material, pH of the dispersion, rate of agitation, swelling time and temperature.

(9) Hydroxyethyl Cellulose (HEC): HEC is partially substituted poly (hydroxyethyl) ether of cellulose. It is obtained by treating alkali cellulose with ethylene oxide. HEC is available as a powder and appears light yellow to white in color. Clear gels are prepared by dissolving HEC in hot or cold water. Dispersions can be prepared quickly by altering the stirring rate of dispersion, temperature and pH.

(10) Hydroxypropyl Cellulose (HPC): HPC is partially substituted poly (hydroxypropyl) ether of cellulose. It is obtained by treating alkali cellulose with propylene oxide at higher temperatures. It is available as tasteless and odorless powder which is yellowish or white in color.

(11) Hydroxypropylmethyl Cellulose (HPMC): HPMC is a partly o-methylated and o-(2-hydroxypropylated) cellulose obtained by treating alkali cellulose with chloromethane and propylene oxide. It is available as odorless and tasteless granular or fibrous powder which is creamy white or white in color. HPMC is soluble in cold water. Aqueous dispersions are prepared by dispersing material in hot water (80°C) under vigorous stirring. On complete hydration of HPMC, a sufficient quantity of cold water is added and mixed. The gel point of HPMC dispersions varies from 50 to 90°C. Gels are stable over a wide pH range (3-11).

(13) Methylcellulose (MC): MC is a long chain cellulose polymer with methoxyl substitutions at positions 2, 3 and 6 of the anhydroglucose ring. It is synthesized by methylating alkali cellulose with methyl chloride. MC is insoluble in hot water but slowly swells and forms viscous colloidal dispersions in cold water. Gels can be prepared by initially mixing the methylcellulose with half the volume of hot water (~ 70°C) followed by addition of the remaining volume of cold water.

Table 4.5 : Gelling Agents

Name	Strength (%) Used
Bentonite	10-20
Carbomer	0.5-2.0
Carboxymethyl cellulose sodium	3.0-6.0
Carrageenan	0.3-2.0
Colloidal silicon dioxide	2.0-10.0

Contd...

Gelatin	10.0-20.0
Glyceryl behenate	1.0-15.0
Guar gum	1.0-5.0
Hydroxypropyl cellulose	2.0-5.0
Hydroxypropylmethyl cellulose	1.0-10.0
Magnesium aluminium silicate	5.0-15.0
Methylcellulose	1.0-5.0
Poloxamer	15.0-20.0
Polyvinyl alcohol	2.5-10.0
Povidone	2.0-20.0
Sodium alginate	10.0-20.0
Tragacanth	1.0-8.0

4.11 PREPARATION AND PACKAGING

Gels are relatively easier to prepare as compared to ointments and creams. In addition to the gelling agent, medicated gels contain drug, antimicrobial preservatives, stabilizers, dispersing agents and permeation enhancers.

Order of Mixing: The order of mixing of these ingredients with the gelling agent is based on their influence on the gelling process. If they are likely to influence the rate and extent of swelling of the gelling agent, they are mixed after the formation of gel. Ideally the drug and other additives are dissolved in the swelling solvent and the swelling agent is added to this solution and allowed to swell.

Gelling Medium: Purified water is the most widely used dispersion medium in the preparation of gels. Under certain circumstances, gels may also contain co-solvents or dispersing agents.

Processing Conditions and Duration of Swelling: The processing temperature, pH of the dispersion and duration of swelling are critical parameters in the preparation of gels. These conditions vary with each gelling agent. Hot water is preferred for gelatin and polyvinyl alcohol, and cold water is preferred for methylcellulose dispersions. Carbomers, guar gum, hydroxypropyl cellulose, poloxamer and tragacanth form gels at weakly acidic or near - neutral pH conditions (pH 5-8). Gelling agents such as carboxy methyl cellulose sodium, hydroxypropylmethyl cellulose and sodium alginate form gels over a wide pH range (4-10). Hydroxyethyl cellulose forms gel at alkaline pH condition. A swelling duration of about 24-48 hours generally helps in obtaining homogeneous gels. Natural gums need about 24 hours and cellulose polymers require about 48 hours for complete hydration.

Removal of Entrapped Air: Entrapment of air bubbles in the gel matrix is a common issue, especially when the swelling process involves a mixing procedure or the drug and other additives are added after the swelling process. Further removal of air bubbles can be achieved by long term standing, low temperature storage, sonication or inclusion of silicon antifoaming agents. In large scale production, vacuum vessel deaerators are used to remove the entrapped air.

Packaging: Being viscous and non - Newtonian systems, gels need high attention during packing into containers. Usually they are packed into squeeze tubes or jars made of plastic materials. Aluminium containers are also used when the product pH is slightly acidic. Pump dispensers and prefilled syringes are sometimes used for packing gels.

Evaluation

Various Pharmacopeial and nonpharmacopeial tests are carried out to evaluate the physicochemical, microbial, in vitro and *in-vivo* characteristics of gels. Some of the tests recommended by the USP for gels include minimum fill, pH, viscosity, microbial screening and assay. In some cases sterility and alcohol content are also specified. Additional tests are carried out such as homogeneity, surface morphology, rheological properties, bioadhesion, stability and *ex-vivo* penetration.

4.12 EVALUATION OF SEMISOLIDS

- Stability of active ingredient and excipients
- Visual appearance : color, odor (development of pungent odor or loss of fragrance)
- Viscosity, extrudability
- Loss of water and other volatile vehicle
- Phase distribution
- Particle size distribution of dispersed phase
- pH
- Texture, feel upon application (stiffness, grittiness, greasiness, tackiness)
- Particulate contamination
- Microbial contamination and sterility (before and after use)
- Release and Bioavailability
- Organoleptic inspection
  - a noticeable change in consistency, such as excessive "bleeding" (separation of excessive amounts of liquid) or formation of agglomerates and grittiness;
  - discoloration;
  - emulsion breakdown;
  - crystal growth;
  - shrinking due to evaporation of water; or
  - evidence of microbial growth.

Some qualitative indicators of chemical instability are, development of color, odor, rancidity while time variable rheological behavior results in physical/chemical changes. Viscometer, rheometer, extrusion rheometer, measures the force it takes to extrude a semisolid through a narrow orifice.

Penetrometers characterize viscosity in terms of the penetration of weighed cone into a semisolid. Brookfield viscometer with spindle and helipath measures the force it takes to drive a spindle helically through a semisolid. Increase/decrease of viscosity by any of the measuring tools indicates change in structural element of the formulation. Changes in product pH also indicate chemical decomposition of hydrolytic nature.

Phase separation or breakage of emulsion indicates acute instability. Bleeding is defined as, the formation of visible droplets of internal phase of an emulsion in the continuum of the semisolid. This problem is due to the slow rearrangement and contraction of internal structure. Here internal phase is squeezed out of the formulation matrix. Storage at warm temperature can induce bleeding so it should be kept in cool place.

4.12.1 Particle Size Distribution and Particulate Nature of Semisolid Suspension

There is consequence of crystal growth; changes in crystalline habit, polymorphic changes etc. and crystalline alteration can lead to a pronounced reduction in the drug delivery compatibility and therapeutic utility of a formulation. This indicates serious physical instability. A more commonly encountered change in formulation is the evaporative loss of water, other volatile phases from a preparation while it is in storage due to inappropriate packaging. Diffusion loss of volatile substance through container walls also occurs.

Such evaporative losses causes a formation to stiffen and become puffy formulation and its application characteristics changes noticeably. There is corresponding weight loss. In some cases, contents of formulation may shrink and pass away from the container wall. Creams and gels mostly suffered due to high fraction of volatile components when stored under warm locations.

Particulate Contamination

The particles should be impalpable/ incapable of being individually perceived by touch, so that formulation does not feel gritty. The palatability of a particle is a function of its hardness, shape and size. Thus it is important to use finely subdivided solid in topical dosage form.

Pharmaceutical Elegance

It covers number of attributes like ease of application, the feel of the preparation once it is on the skin and appearance of the applied skin. The ease of application and method of application of a formulation depends on the physicochemical attitudes of the system involved. The spreadability is a rheological quality related to the nature and degree of internal structure of the formulation. Paste is very stiff and hard to apply; their application over broken and irritated skin can be disagreeable. Tackiness and greasiness are determined by the physiochemical properties of the vehicle constituents that comprise the formed film in the skin.

4.12.2 Skin Irritation Tests

1. 21 Days cumulative irritation study

The test compound is applied mainly to the same site on the back or forearm. Test materials are applied under occlusive tape and scores are read daily. The test application and scoring are repeated daily for 21 days or until irritation produces a predetermined maximum score. Usually 24 subjects are used. Fewer substance and shorter application time in day are variants of the test.

Table 4.6 : Skin Irritation Test

Score	Inference
0	no visible reaction
1	mild erythema
2	intense erythema
3	intense erythema with edema
4	intense erythema with edema and vesicular erosion

2. Draize–Shelanski Repeat–Insult Patch Test

This test is performed to measure the potential to cause sensitization and irritancy potential. In the usual procedure the test material or a suitable dilution is applied under occlusion to the same site for 10 alternative days for 24 hours periods. Following a 7 day rest period the test material is applied again to fresh site for 24 hours. The challenge sites are read on removal of the patch and again 24 hours later. The 0-4 erythema scale is used. A test panel of 100 individuals is common.

3. Kligman Maximization Test

This test is used to detect the contact sensitizing potential of a product or material. The test material is applied under occlusion to the same site for 48 hours period. Prior to each exposure the site may be pretreated with a solution of SLS under occlusion. Following 10 days interval the test material again is applied to the different site for 48 hours, under occlusion. The change site may be treated briefly with a SLS solution. This test is of shorter duration and makes use of fewer test subjects. The use of SLS as a pretreatment increases the ability to detect weaker allergens. This result however does not disqualify the use of a substance as unsafe. The actual risk of use depends on concentration, period at use and skin condition.

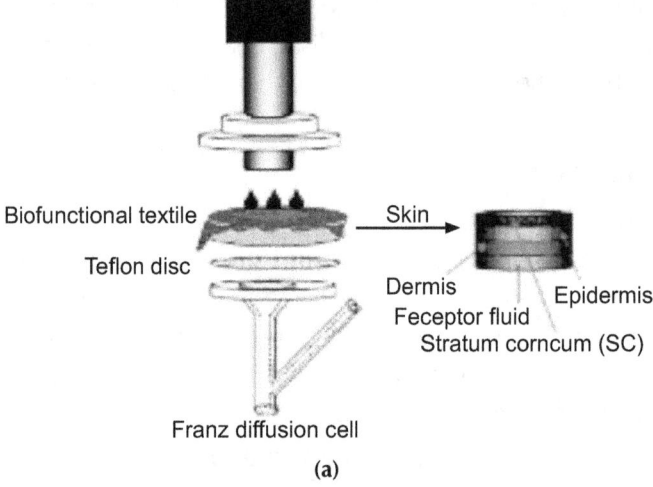

(a)

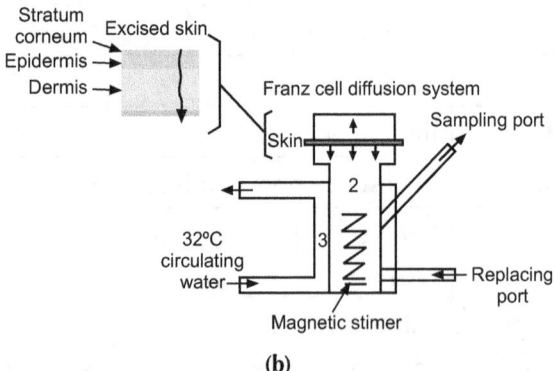

(b)

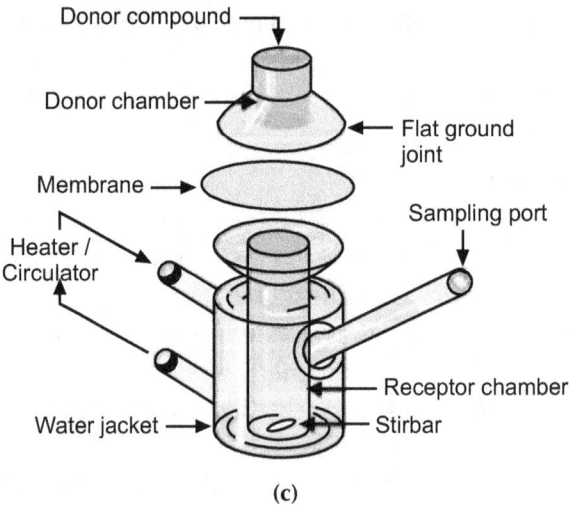

(c)

Fig. 4.11 : Specimen Diffusion Cell

4.12.3 Measurement of Skin Absorption

Direct measurement

In-vivo

This can be done in animals or humans with a dry chemical powder or a chemical in solution. Rats are commonly used for these experiments. An area of skin is shaved before the chemical is applied. Often the area of chemical application is covered to prevent ingestion or rubbing off of the test material. Samples of blood and urine are taken at specific time intervals following application (0.5, 1, 2, 4, 10, and 24 hours) and in some protocols at the chosen end time the animal may be sacrificed and tissue samples may also be evaluated for the presence of the test chemical.

Ex-vivo

Skin can be removed carefully from animals and used to see the extent of local penetration by putting it in a chamber and applying the chemical on one side and then measuring the amount of chemical that gets into a fluid on the other side.

In-vitro

Techniques such as static diffusion cells (Franz cells) and flow through diffusion cells have also been used. The Franz cell apparatus consists of two chambers separated by a membrane of animal or human skin. The test product is applied to the membrane via the top chamber. The bottom chamber contains fluid from which samples are taken at regular intervals for analysis to determine the amount of active that has permeated the membrane at set time points. Flow through diffusion cells is similar to Franz cells.

4.13 LABELLING AND PLANT LAYOUT

Every pharmaceutical preparation must comply with the labelling requirements established under Good Manufacturing Practice.

The label should include:

(1) The name of the pharmaceutical product;

(2) The name(s) of the active ingredient(s);

(3) The amount of the active ingredient(s) in a specified quantity of suitable base or vehicle, and the quantity of preparation in the container;

(4) The batch (lot) number assigned by the manufacturer;

(5) The expiry date and, when required, the date of manufacture;

(6) Any special storage conditions or handling precautions that may be necessary;

(7) Directions for use, warnings, and precautions that may be necessary;

(8) The name and address of the manufacturer or the person responsible for placing the product on the market;

(9) The name and quantity of antimicrobial agent incorporated in the preparation; and

(10) If applicable, the statement that the preparation is "sterile".

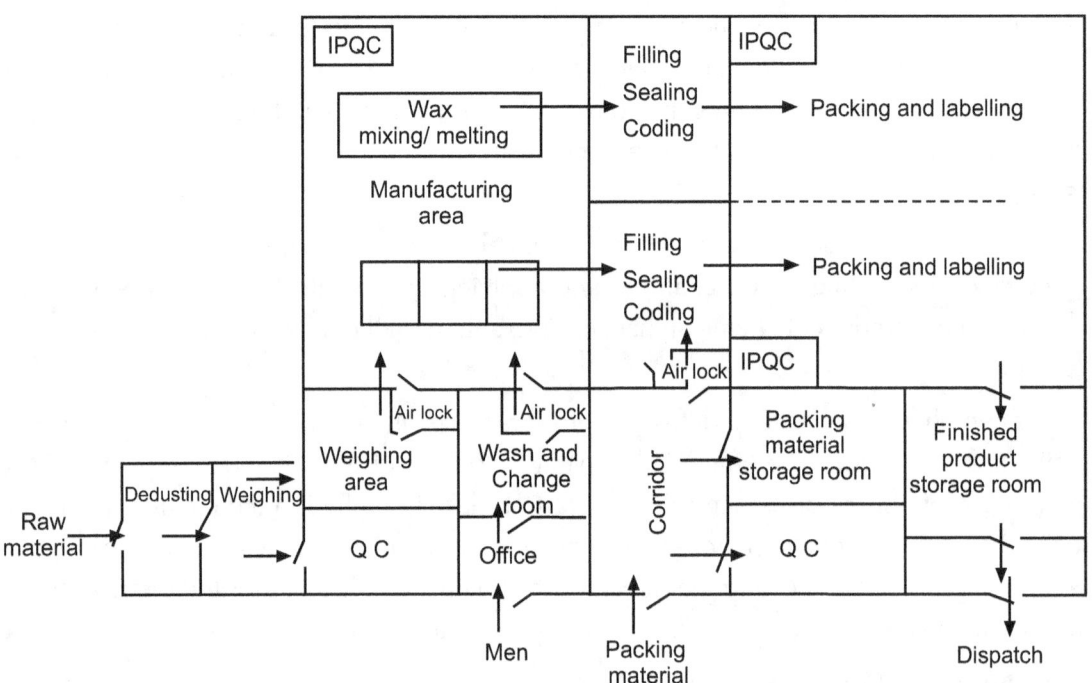

Fig. 4.12: Plant Layout

❖ ❖ ❖

CHAPTER 5...

MANUFACTURING EQUIPMENTS

Manufacturing Equipments for suspensions, emulsion and semisolids are discussed in previous chapters.

Equipments used in Manufacturing Suspensions

- Fluid Energy Mill 2.5.1; pg. no. 2.8
- Ball Mill 2.5.2; pg. no. 2.9
- Micronizer 2.5.3; pg. no. 2.10
- Edge Runner Mill 2.5.4; pg. no. 2.11
- Hammer Mill 2.5.5; pg. no. 2.12
- Roller Mill 2.5.6; pg. no. 2.13

Equipments used in Manufacturing Emulsions

- Agitators 3.14.1; pg. no. 3.21
- Mechanical Mixers 3.14.2; pg. no. 3.21
- Colloid Mills 3.14.3; pg. no. 3.22
- Homogenizers 3.14.4; pg. no. 3.23
- Ultrasonic Devices 3.14.5; pg. no. 3.25

Equipments used in Manufacturing Semisolids

- Planetary Motion Mixers 4.8; pg. no. 4.20
- Colloid Mill 4.8; pg. no. 4.20
- Sigma Blender 4.8; pg. no. 4.21
- Three Roll Mill 4.8; pg. no. 4.22

Time : 3 Hours]   Max. Marks :70

Instructions to the candidates:

1) *All questions are compulsory.*

2) *Answers to the two sections should be written in separate answer books.*

3) *Neat labelled diagrams must be drawn wherever necessary.*

4) *Figures to the right indicate full marks.*

SECTION - I

Q1) Explain the principle and factors influencing development of a stable antacid suspension of combined Aluminium hydroxide paste and Magnesium hydroxide gel.   **[10]**

OR

Explain stability of suspensions and describe in detail role of particle size, density and viscosity in development of a stable suspension.

Q2) **Answer the following (Any 5)**   **[15]**

a) Describe the molecular basis of surface tension affecting manufacturing of emulsion.

b) With the help of its neat labelled diagram, describe the role of ultrasonifiers in manufacturing of disperse systems.

c) Enlist the quality control parameters of emulsions. Describe any one in detail.

d) Explain the concept of phase inversion temperature.

e) Describe briefly the structured vehicle concept.

f) What is wetting? How wettability of solids is measured? What is the role of wetting in manufacturing of emulsions?

g) Describe layout for manufacturing of disperse system as per Schedule M.

Q3) **Write short notes on (Any two)**   **[10]**

a) Identification test for type of emulsion

b) Multiple emulsion

c) Packaging and labelling of Suspension

d) Acid neutralizing capacity (As per USP).

SECTION - II

Q4) Describe various routes a drug substance may take to penetrate the skin.   **[10]**

OR

Describe the *in vitro* and *in vivo* methods for studying drug diffusion through skin.

Q5) **Answer the following (Any 5)**   **[15]**

a) How is the spreadability of dermatological preparations evaluated?

    b)   "One point viscometers are useless to study rheology of dermatologicals" explain.

    c)   "Mixed emulsifier systems for dermatologicals give better results than single emulsifier systems"- explain.

    d)   How low energy emulsification may be useful in saving energy during manufacturing of dermatologicals?

    e)   Write in brief about 'emulsified ointment bases'.

    f)   Discuss different types of antioxidants used in dermatologicals.

    g)   How the safety and efficacy testing of dermatologicals is done?

Q6) **Write short notes on (Any two)**   **[10]**

    a)   Penetration enhancers

    b)   Properties of gels

    c)   Viscosity evaluation of dermatologicals

    d)   Equipments in manufacturing of semisolids.

OCTOBER 2016

Time : 3 Hours]   Max. Marks :70

Instructions to the candidates:

1) *All questions are compulsory.*

2) *Answers to the two sections should be written in separate answer books.*

3) *Neat labeled diagrams must be drawn wherever necessary.*

4) *Figures to the right indicate full marks.*

SECTION - I

Q1) Write about various approaches adopted to stabilize suspensions. Add a note on wetting. **[10]**

OR

What are instabilities of emulsion? Explain in detail reasons and precaution measures to avoid instability of emulsion.

Q2) **Answer the following (Any 5)**   **[15]**

   a)   Enlist and explain identification test for type of emulsion.

   b)   Explain in detail suspensions for reconstitution.

   c)   Describe different drug release mechanisms from emulsion as a dosage form.

   d)   Write a note on formulation of suspensions based on low and high solid content.

   e)   Describe layout for manufacturing of suspension as per Schedule M.

   f)   Explain in detail concept Thermodynamic vs Kinetic stability of dispersed systems.

   g)   Enlist and describe in detail any one method for manufacturing of multiple emulsion.

Q3) **Write short notes on (Any two)**   **[10]**

   a)   Preservatives in emulsions

   b)   Controlled flocculation

   c)   Role of HLB in selection of emulsifying agent

   d)   Stoke's law in relation with stability of suspension.

SECTION - II

Q4) Give a detail account of evaluation of dermatologicals.   **[10]**

OR

Give an account of routes of percutaneous absorption of durgs.

Q5) **Answer the following (Any 5)**   **[15]**

   a)   Describe the role of electrolytes in stabilizing an emulsion.

   b)   What are diffusion cells? What is their use in evaluation of dermatological preparations?

   c)   "Methyl paraben and propyl paraben is used in combination in dermatological preparations' explain.

   d) What are emollients and humectants? What is their use in dermatological preparations?

   e) What is phase inversion temperature? Why an emulsion that undergoes phase inversion has better stability?

   f) What are the different types of structures observed in gels?

   g) How spreadability and stickiness of a dermatological preparation is evaluated?

Q6) **Write short notes on (Any two)**   **[10]**

   a) Types of ointment bases

   b) Penetration enhancers

   c) Antioxidants in dermatological formulations

   d) Gel forming agents.

BIBLIOGRAPHY

➢ L V Allen, N G Popovich, H C Ansel, Ansel's Pharmaceutical dosage forms & Drug Delivery Systems, 9th edition, 2nd Indian reprint, 2011, Published by Lippincott Williams and Wilkins, Wolters Kluwer (India) Pvt. Ltd., New Delhi.

➢ M E Aulton, K Taylor, Pharmaceutics: The Science of Dosage Form Design, 2nd edition. Edited by M E Aulton, Published by Churchill Livingstone, 2001.

➢ Remington: The Science and Practice of Pharmacy, Volumes 1-2, 22nd edition, 2012, Edited by Allen L V, Adeboye A, Shane P D, Linda A F, Jointly published by Pharmaceutical Press and Philadelphia College of Pharmacy at University of the Sciences.

➢ Leon Lachman, Herbert A. Lieberman, Joseph L. Kanig, the Theory and Practice of Industrial Pharmacy. 3rd edition, 1986, CBS Publishers and Distributors, New Delhi.

➢ G S Banker and C T Rhodes , Modern Pharmaceutics, 4th edition, revised and expanded, 2009, Edited by G S Banker and C T Rhodes, Published by Informa Healthcare USA Inc. New York.

➢ A R Paradkar, Introduction to Pharmaceutical Engineering, 10th edition, 2007, Published by Nirali Prakashan, Pune.

➢ Indian Pharmacopoeia, 2010, Volumes I, II & III, Published by The Indian Pharmacopoeia Commission, Ghaziabad, Government of India, Ministry of Health & Family Welfare.

➢ British Pharmacopoeia, 2009, Volumes I-IV and Veterinary, Published by British Pharmacopoeia Commission, the Stationary Office on behalf of Medicines and Healthcare products Regulatory Agency (MHRA), United Kingdom.

➢ United States Pharmacopeia 35 - National Formulary 30 by United States Pharmacopeia Convention, Volumes I-3.

INDEX

A

Absorption Base, 4.10, 4.11, 4.14

Acacia, 3.5, 3.17, 3.18, 3.20

Ageing, 3.30

Agitation, 3.2-3.4, 3.12, 3.21, 3.31, 3.34

Agitator, 3.21

Amphoteric, 3.15, 3.16

Anionic Surfactant, 3.15

Antioxidants, 3.19

B

Attraction, 1.2

Auxiliary Emulsifying Agents, 3.18

Ball Mill, 2.9

Bancroft's Rule, 3.14

Beaker Method, 3.21

Bentonite, 3.6, 3.15, 3.18

Bottle Method, 3.21

Breaking, 3.3, 3.11, 3.13, 3.20, 3.31, 3.33

Buffers, 2.15

C

Caking, 2.16-2.17

Carbomer, 4.15, 4.26, 4.27, 4.28

Cationic Surfactant, 3.12, 3.13, 3.15

Cellulose Derivatives, 3.5, 3.17

Centrifugation, 3.30-3.31

Cloud Point, 3.8

Coagulation, 3.33

Coalescence, 3.2-3.5, 3.9, 3.11-3.13, 3.17, 3.26, 3.30, 3.33, 3.35

Colloidal Mill, 3.24

Colorants, 2.15

Comminution, 1.1, 3.19

Controlled Flocculation, 2.16, 2.17

Creaming, 3.9, 3.11, 3.13, 3.19, 3.30, 3.33, 3.34

Crystal Growth, 2.19, 2.20

Coulter Counter, 3.36

D

Density Modifier, 3.19

Diffusion Cell, 3.32, 3.33

Disperse Systems, 1.1, 3.38

Dispersion, 3.2, 3.11, 3.12, 3.15, 3.21, 3.23, 3.33

DLVO Theory, 1.2

Draize–Shelanski Repeat–Insult Patch Test, 4.31

Dry Gum Method, 3.20

Dry Suspensions for Reconstitution, 2.20

E

Edge Runner Mill, 2.11

Electrical Double Layer, 3.4, 3.9, 3.26

Electro Neutrality, 2.7

Electrokinetic Properties, 2.7

Electrolyte, 2.16, 2.18

Electrophoretic Properties, 3.33

Electrostatic Repulsion, 3.5, 3.17

Emulgents, 3.12, 3.14, 3.31

Emulsion Stabilizations, 3.4

Energy Barrier, 3.9

Equipments for Emulsion Manufacturing, 3.21

Equipments for Suspension Manufacturing, 2.8

Ex Vivo, 4.29

Excipients Used in Suspensions, 2.14

F

Factors Affecting Percutaneous Absorption, 4.8

Fick's Law, 4.8

Flavor, 2.15

Flocculated and Deflocculated System, 2.3

Flocculating Agents, 2.17

Flocculation, 2.3, 2.5, 2.7

Fluid Energy Mill, 2.8

Free Energy Consideration, 1.1

Fusion Method, 4.19

Gels And Jellies, 4.6

Gravitation, 3.30

Griffin Scale, 3.7

Hammer Mill, 2.12

Hlb, 3.3, 3.4, 3.7, 3.13, 3.14

Homogenizers, 3.23

Humectants, 3.18

Hydrophilic Colloids, 3.17, 3.33

Hydroxy Propyl Cellulose, 4.27

Hydroxy Propyl Methyl Cellulose, 4.27

Interfacial Film, 3.4, 3.5, 3.9

Interfacial Tension, 3.15, 3.17

In-Vitro, 4.29

In-Vivo, 4.29

Kligman, 4.31

Kraft Point, 3.8

Lanolin, 4.11

London Type, 1.2

Low Energy Emulsification, 3.4

Lyophobic Colloids, 1.2

Mechanical Mixer, 3.21

Micro Emulsion, 3.27

Microcrystalline Wax, 4.13

Micronizer, 2.10

Minimum Fill, 4.29

Monomolecular Film, 3.15

Multimolecular Film, 3.16

Multiple Emulsion, 3.25

Nernst Potential, 2.7

Non-Ionic Surfactant, 3.16

Ointment Bases, 4.10

Oleaginous Bases, 4.10

Ostwald Ripening, 3.8

P

Particle Properties, 1.4

Partition Coefficient, 4.10

Penetration Enhancers, 4.14

Percutaneous Absorption, 4.7

Phase Inversion Temperature (PIT), 3.3, 3.27

Phase Inversion, 3.13

Phase Viscosity, 3.9

Planetary Mixer, 4.20

Polyethylene Glycols, 4.12

Polymorphism, 2.19

Potential Energy, 1.2

Preservatives, 3.19

Process Parameters, 4.10

Propeller Mixer, 3.22

Protective Colloids, 2.14, 2.17

Redispersability, 2.6

Repulsion, 1.2

Roller Mill, 2.13

Schulman- Cockbain Theory, 3.5

Sedimentation Parameters, 2.4

Sedimentation Volume, 2.5

Semi Synthetic Polysaccharide, 3.17

Shelf Life, 3.30

Sigma Blender, 4.21

Skin- Irritation Test, 4.31

Sodium CMC, 4.26

Span, 3.7, 3.16

Stability Testing, 3.30

Steric Repulsion, 3.10

Stoke's Law, 3.11

Stress Conditions, 3.30

Structured Vehicle, 2.17

Techniques of Emulsification, 3.19

Theory of Emulsification, 3.4

Theory of Sedimentation, 2.3

Thermodynamic Stability, 3.28

Timing, 3.4

Total Energy, 1.2

Triple Roller Mill, 4.22

Trituration Method, 4.19

Tweens, 3.7

Ultrasonic Device, 3.25

Van Der Wall Attraction, 1.2

Water Removable Bases, 4.11

Water Soluble Bases, 4.11

Wet Gum Method, 3.20

Wetting Agent, 2.15

White Bees Wax, 4.13

Yellow Bees Wax, 4.13

Zeta Potential, 2.7

www.ingramcontent.com/pod-product-compliance
Lightning Source LLC
Chambersburg PA
CBHW081325020726
47506CB00005B/1176